This book belongs to

Alice Kirkhope

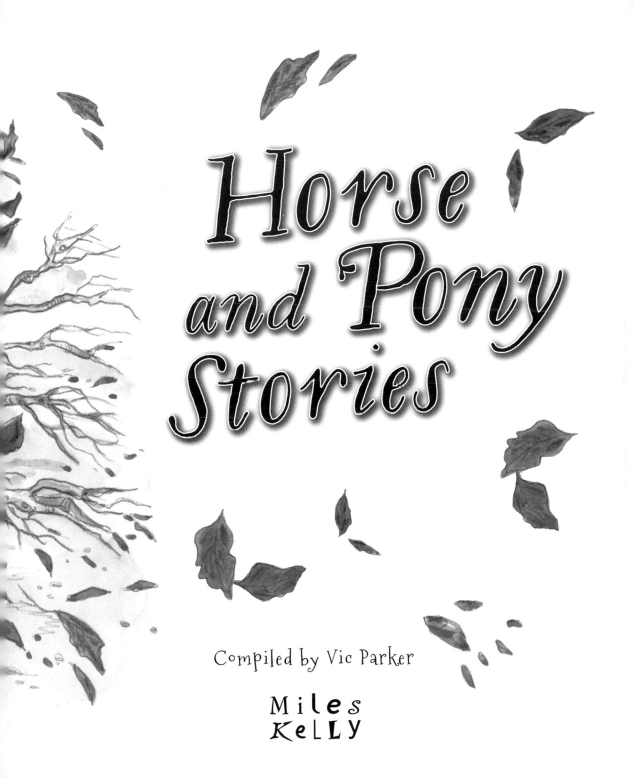

Horse and Pony Stories

Compiled by Vic Parker

Miles Kelly

First published in 2013 by Miles Kelly Publishing Ltd
Harding's Barn, Bardfield End Green, Thaxted, Essex, CM6 3PX, UK

Copyright © Miles Kelly Publishing Ltd 2013

This edition printed 2016

6 8 10 9 7 5

Publishing Director Belinda Gallagher
Creative Director Jo Cowan
Editorial Director Rosie Neave
Senior Editor Claire Philip
Designer Rob Hale
Production Elizabeth Collins, Caroline Kelly
Reprographics Stephan Davis, Jennifer Cozens, Thom Allaway
Assets Lorraine King

ISBN 978-1-78617-077-4

Printed in China

British Library Cataloguing-in-Publication Data
A catalogue record for this book is available from the British Library

ACKNOWLEDGEMENTS
The publishers would like to thank the following artists who have contributed to this book:

The Bright Agency: Jessica Courtney-Tickle (cover), Mélanie Florian,
Kirsteen Harris-Jones (inc. borders)
Beehive Illustration: Iole Rosa, Gail Yerrill
Frank Endersby

Made with paper from a sustainable forest

www.mileskelly.net

CONTENTS

INTO THE SADDLE

NOBLE STEEDS

RIDE LIKE THE WIND

ADVENTURES ON HORSEBACK

HOME FREE

10

INTO THE SADDLE

My Breaking In

From *Black Beauty* by Anna Sewell

Anna Sewell was the first person to write a novel from a horse's point of view. Her story is set in Victorian Britain, and it showed how difficult a horse's life could be. The story begins with an account of Black Beauty as a foal. He lived on a farm with his mother and some other young horses.

I WAS GROWING UP. My coat had become fine and soft, and was bright black. I had one white foot and a pretty white star on my forehead. I was thought very handsome.

My master would not sell me till I was four years old – he said lads ought not to work like men and colts ought not to work like horses till they were quite grown up.

When I was four years old, Squire Gordon came to look at me. He examined my eyes, my mouth and my legs. He felt them all down, and then I had to walk and trot and gallop before him. He seemed to like me, and said, "When he has been well broken in, he will do very well."

My master said he would break me in himself, as he did not want me to be frightened or hurt – and he lost no time about it, for the next day he began.

Everyone may not know what breaking in is, therefore I will describe it. It means to teach a horse to wear a saddle and bridle, and to carry on his back a man, woman or child, to go just the way they wish, and to go quietly. Besides this he has to learn to have a cart fixed behind him, so that he cannot walk or trot without dragging it after him, and he must go fast or slow, just as his driver wishes.

He must never startle at what he sees, nor speak to other horses, nor bite, nor kick. He must not have any will of his own, but always do his master's will, even though he may be very tired or hungry. The worst of all is, when his harness is on, he may neither jump for joy nor lie down for weariness. So you see, this breaking in is a big thing.

I had long been used to a halter, and being led about in the fields and lanes but now I was to have a bit and bridle.

My Breaking In

That day, my master gave me some oats as usual. Then, after a good deal of coaxing, he got the bit into my mouth and the bridle fixed – but it was a nasty thing!

Those who have never had a bit in their mouths cannot think how bad it feels. A great piece of cold, hard steel as thick as a man's finger to be pushed into one's mouth, between one's teeth, and over one's tongue, with the ends coming out at the corner of your mouth, and held fast there by straps over your head, under your throat, round your nose, and under your chin, so that no way in the world can you get rid of the nasty hard thing. It is very bad! Yes, very bad! At least I thought so, but I knew my mother always wore one when she went out, and all horses did when they were grown up. And so, what with the nice oats, and what with my master's pats, kind words, and gentle ways, I got to wear my bit and bridle.

Next came the saddle, but that was not half so bad. My master put it on my back very gently, while Daniel held my head. He then made the girths fast under my body, patting and talking to me all the time.

I had a few oats, then a little leading about. And this he did every day till I began to look for the oats and the saddle. At length, one morning, my master

got on my back and rode me round the
meadow on the soft grass. It certainly did
feel queer, but I must say I felt rather proud
to carry my master and, as he continued to
ride me a little every day, I soon got
used to it.

The next unpleasant
business was putting on the
iron shoes – that too was very
hard at first. My master went
with me to the smith's forge,
to see that I was not hurt or
frightened. The blacksmith
took my feet in his hand, one
after the other, and cut away
some of the hoof – it did not
pain me, so I stood still on

three legs till he had done them all. Then he took a piece of iron the shape of my foot and clapped it on, and drove some nails through the shoe into my hoof, so that the shoe was firmly on. My feet felt very stiff and heavy, but in time I got used to it.

Having got so far, there were more new things to wear. First, a stiff heavy collar on my neck, and a bridle with great side-pieces against my eyes called blinkers – and blinkers indeed they were, for I could not see on either side – only straight in front.

Next, there was a small saddle with a nasty stiff strap that went right under my tail – that was the crupper. I hated the crupper! To have my long tail doubled up and poked through that strap was almost as

bad as the bit. I never felt more like kicking, but of course I could not kick such a good master, and so in time I got used to everything and could do my work as well as my mother.

I must not forget to mention one part of my training, which was a very great help. My master sent me for a fortnight to a neighbouring farm, where there was a meadow skirted on one side by the railway. I was turned in here, among some sheep and cows.

I shall never forget the first train that ran by. I was feeding quietly near the railway fence when I heard a strange sound. It was in the distance, but before I could work out where it was coming from, there was a rush

INTO THE SADDLE

and a clatter and a puffing out of smoke –
a long black train of something flew by and
was gone almost before I could draw my
breath. I turned and galloped to the far side
of the meadow as fast as I could go and
there I stood snorting with surprise.

My Breaking In

   During the day many other trains went
by, some more slowly. These drew up at the
station close by and sometimes made an
awful shriek and groan before they stopped.
I thought it very dreadful, but the cows
went on eating quietly and hardly raised
their heads as the black frightful thing came
puffing and grinding past.

   For the first few days I could not feed in
peace, but as I found that this terrible
creature never came into the field, or did
me any harm, I began to disregard it, and
very soon I cared as little about the passing
of a train as the cows and sheep did.

   Since then I have seen many horses
much alarmed and startled at the sight or
sound of a steam engine, but thanks to my

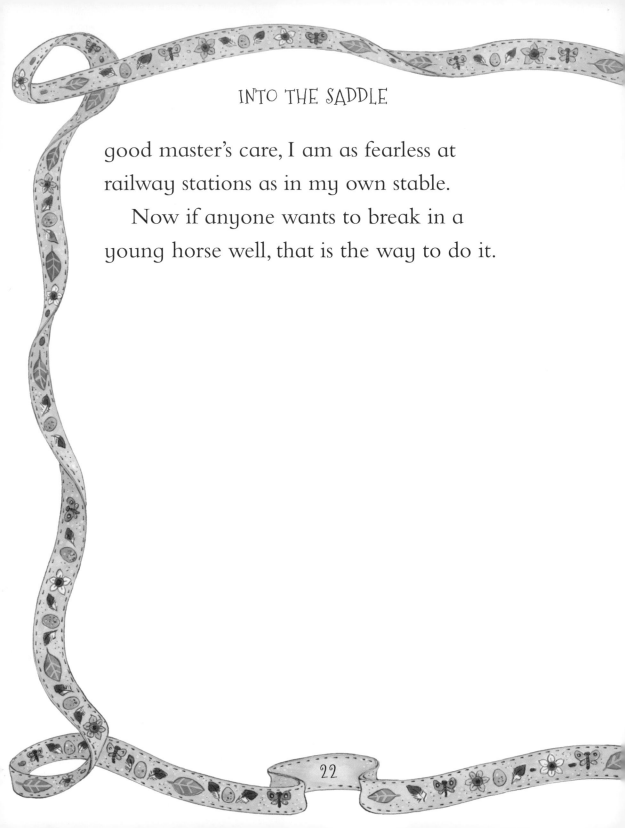

good master's care, I am as fearless at railway stations as in my own stable.

Now if anyone wants to break in a young horse well, that is the way to do it.

Alice and the White Knight

From *Through the Looking-glass* by Lewis Carroll

In this story, a young girl called Alice falls through a mirror into a back-to-front world full of chess pieces. After many magical adventures, she comes across a knight with an unusual problem…

ALICE WALKED ON IN SILENCE, every now and then stopping to help the poor knight, who certainly was not a good rider. Whenever the horse stopped, which it did very often, he fell off in front, and whenever it went on again, which it generally did rather suddenly, he fell off behind.

Otherwise he stayed on pretty well, except that he had a habit of now and then falling off sideways, and, as he generally did this on the side on which Alice was walking, she soon found that it was the best plan not to walk quite so close to the horse.

"I'm afraid you've not had much practice in riding," she ventured to say as she was helping him up after yet another tumble to the ground.

The knight looked very much surprised and a little offended at the remark. "What makes you say that?" he asked, as he scrambled back into the saddle, keeping hold of Alice's hair with one hand, to save himself from falling over on the other side.

"Because people don't fall off so often,

when they've had practice."

"I've had plenty of practice," the knight said very gravely, "plenty of practice!"

Alice could think of nothing better to say than, "Indeed?" but she said it as heartily as she could. They went on a little way in silence after this, the knight with his eyes shut, muttering to himself.

"The great art of riding," the knight suddenly began in a loud voice, waving his right arm as he spoke, "is to keep—" Here the sentence ended, as the knight fell heavily on the top of his head.

Alice was quite frightened this time and said in an anxious tone, as she picked him up, "I hope no bones are broken?"

"None to speak of," the knight said. "The

great art of riding, as I was saying, is to keep your balance properly. Like this…"

He let go of the bridle and stretched out both his arms to show Alice what he meant – and this time he fell off the horse and landed right under the horse's feet.

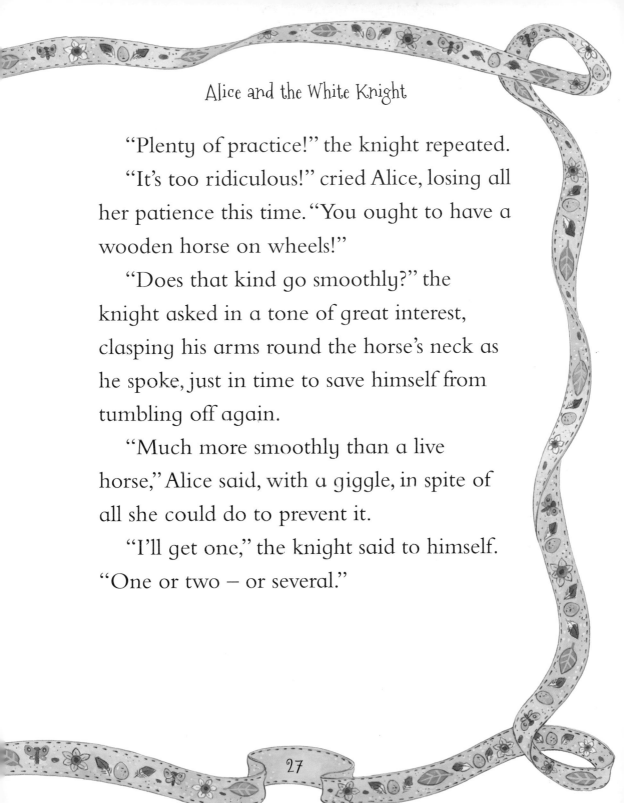

"Plenty of practice!" the knight repeated.

"It's too ridiculous!" cried Alice, losing all her patience this time. "You ought to have a wooden horse on wheels!"

"Does that kind go smoothly?" the knight asked in a tone of great interest, clasping his arms round the horse's neck as he spoke, just in time to save himself from tumbling off again.

"Much more smoothly than a live horse," Alice said, with a giggle, in spite of all she could do to prevent it.

"I'll get one," the knight said to himself. "One or two — or several."

The Ponies of the Plains

From *Long Lance* by Chief Buffalo Child Long Lance

The birth name of Chief Buffalo Child Long Lance was Sylvester Clark Long. He was an American writer, journalist and actor who lived around a hundred years ago. He was descended from Native Americans.

WITH THE FIRST TOUCH OF SPRING, we broke camp and headed south-west across the big bend of the upper River Columbia, towards the high, flat ground between the Rocky and Cascades mountains. It was here that the world's largest herd of wild horses had roamed during the last hundred and fifty years. It was these horses that we were after, to replace the herd that the storm had driven away from our camp.

We found them in early spring, after the horses had got their first good feed of green grass, and their speed had been slowed by stomach-ache.

There they were – a herd of about five hundred animals, grazing away on the side of a craggy little mountain. Their quick, alert movements, more like those of a deer than those of a horse, showed they were highly-strung beings that would dash off into space like a flock of wild birds if given the slightest cause for excitement.

INTO THE SADDLE

There was one big, steel-dust stallion who grazed away from the rest and made frequent trips along the edge of the herd. It was obvious to our braves that this iron-coloured fellow with the silver mane was the stallion who ruled the herd.

Our warriors directed all of their attention to him, knowing that the movements of the entire herd depended on what he did. Our braves began to make little noises, so that the horses could see us in the distance, and would not be taken by surprise and frightened into a stampede. "Hoh!" our braves grunted softly.

The steel-dust stallion uttered a low whinny. All the herd raised their heads high into the air and, standing perfectly still

as though charmed,
looked intently over
at us with their big,
nervous nostrils
wide open.

They stood that
way for moments,
without moving a muscle, looking
hard at us. Then, as we came too
near, the burly stallion tried to put fear
into us by dashing straight at us with a
deep, rasping roar.

Others followed him, and on they came
like a yelling war party, their heads
swinging wildly, their racing legs wide and
their long tails lashing from side to side.

Before they reached us, the speeding

animals stiffened their legs and came to a
sudden halt in a cloud of dust. While they
were close, they took one more good look
at us, and then they turned and scampered
away over the brow of the mountain.

But the big steel-dust stallion stood his
ground alone for a moment and openly
defied us. He dug his front feet into the dirt
far out in front of him, wagged his head
furiously. Around he jumped gracefully into
the air, swapping ends like a dog chasing its
tail. Then again he raised his head high
and, with his long silver tail lying over his
back, he blazed fire at us through the whites
of his flint-coloured eyes. Having displayed
to us his courage, his defiance and his
leadership, he now turned and pranced off,

with heels flying so high and lightly that one could almost imagine he was treading air.

For ten days we chased this huge family of wild horses. Then came the big night, the night that we were going to capture this great, stubborn herd. No one went to bed that evening. Shortly before nightfall, more than half of our braves quietly slipped out of our camp and disappeared.

They fanned out to the right and crept noiselessly towards the place where the herd had disappeared that afternoon. We heard wolves calling to one another. Arctic owls, night hawks and panthers were crying out mournfully in the darkness. They were our men's signals informing one another of their movements.

Then, about midnight, everything became deathly quiet. We knew that they had located the herd and surrounded it, and that they were now lying on their bellies, awaiting the first streaks of dawn and the signal to start the drive.

Next, Chief Mountain Elk went through our camp, quietly giving instructions for all hands to line themselves along a runway we had made, ready to beat in the herd. Every woman, old person, and child in the camp was called up to take part. This was important work, and everyone had to help.

The children and the women crept over to the runway and sprawled along the outside of the fence, while the men went beyond the fenced part of the runway and hid themselves behind the brush and logs, where it was a little more dangerous.

We crouched low down on the ground and shivered quietly for what felt like hours before we heard a distant, "Ho! Ho! Ho!" It was the muffled driving cry of our warriors.

For ten days they had been uttering this call to the horses to let them know that no harm could come to them from this sound, so the horses did not stampede, as they might have done if taken by surprise by a strange noise.

We youngsters lay breathless in expectancy. The thrill of the wait was almost too much! Each of us had picked out our favourite mounts in this beautiful herd of wild animals. Our fathers had all promised us that after we had caught them we could keep the ponies that we had picked, and we could hardly wait to get our hands on them.

My favourite animal was a beautiful calico pony – a roan, white and red pinto. I thought it was the best and most beautiful of the whole herd. The three different colours were splashed on his shoulders and flanks like a quilt of exquisite design.

Presently we heard the distant rumble of horses' hooves – a dull booming that shook the ground on which we lay, eagerly watching and waiting.

Then all of a sudden, "Yip-yip-yip, he-heeh-h-h!" came the night call of the wolf from many different directions. We heard the call again, "Yip-yip-yip, he-heeh-h-h!"

It was our braves signalling to one another to keep the herd on the right path.

From out of this medley of odd sounds,

we could hear the mares calling their little long-legged sons to their sides so that they might not become lost in the darkness of the night.

Our boyish hearts began to beat fast when we heard the first loud call, "Yah! Yah! Yah!" We knew straight away that action was taking place, and that the herd had now entered the runway. Our warriors were jumping up from their hiding-places and showing themselves with fierce noises, in order to stampede the horses and send them racing headlong into our camp.

Immediately there was a loud thunder of hooves. The horses were running around in great confusion. Above this din of bellowing throats and hammering feet, we heard one loud, full, deep-chested roar, which we all recognized, and it gave us boys a slight thrill of fear. It sounded like a cross between the roar of a lion and the bellow of an infuriated bull.

It was the massive steel-dust stallion, the furious king of the herd. In our imagination we could see his long silver tail thrown over his back, his legs lashing wide apart, and stark anger glistening from the whites of those incredible eyes. We wondered what he would do if he should crash through that fence into our midst.

But then, here he came, leading his raging herd, and we had no further time to think about danger. Our job was to do as the others had done all along the line – to lie still and wait until the lead stallion had passed us, and then to climb up to the top of the fence and yell and wave with all the ferocity that we could command. This was to keep the herd from crashing straight into the fence or trying to turn around, and to hasten their speed into our camp.

Therump, therump, therump! On came the loud, storming herd, *Therump, therump, therump!*

And as we youngsters peeped through the brush-covered fences, we could see their sleek backs bobbing up and down in the starlit darkness like great billows of raging water. The turbulent steel-dust stallion was leading them with front feet wide apart. His death-dealing heels were swinging to the

right and left with each savage leap of his mighty frame.

As the horses thundered closer, the steel-grey stallion stretched himself past us like a huge greyhound, and with each incredible leap, he panted a breath that shrieked like a loud whistle.

And then a few seconds later the rest of the heard came booming past us. I thought that herd would never stop! I had never seen so many horses before, it seemed. On and on they kept coming, galloping past as if they would never stop. We soon lost count of the numbers, there were just too many! We stuck to our posts until it was nearly daylight, and still they came…

Four months later, we were again back

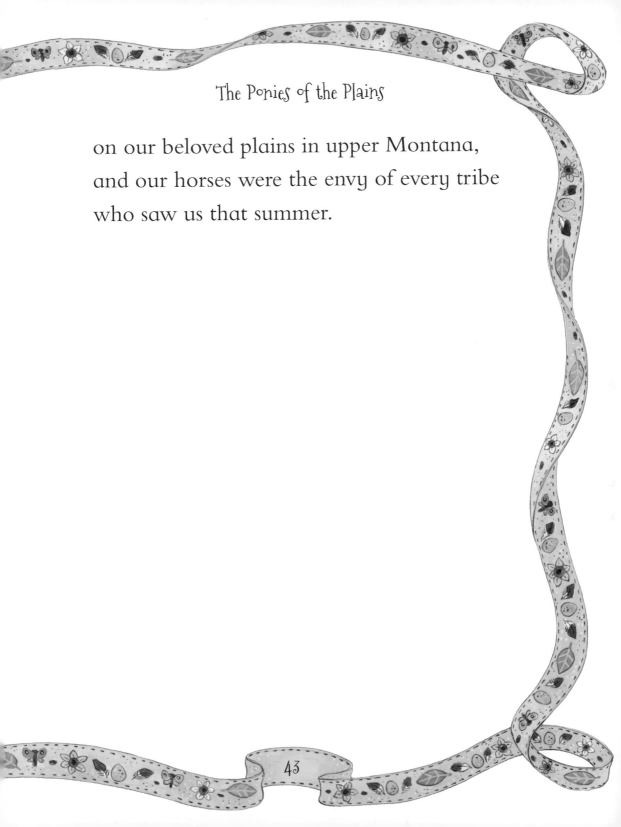

on our beloved plains in upper Montana,
and our horses were the envy of every tribe
who saw us that summer.

Taken for a Ride

From *The Talking Horse* by F Anstey

During the Victorian period, some fashionable wealthy people liked to ride horses down Rotten Row, a track in Hyde Park, London. In this story, a young man called Gustavus Pulvertoft wants to join them. He learns to ride, but with with unexpected results…

I ATTENDED A FASHIONABLE riding-school near Hyde Park, determined to acquire the art of horsemanship.

To say that I found learning a pleasure would be a lie. I have passed many happier hours than those I spent cantering round four bare whitewashed walls on a snorting horse, with my stirrups crossed upon the saddle. The riding-master informed me from time to time that I was getting on – and I knew instinctively when I was coming off – but I must have made some progress, for as time went on he became more and more encouraging.

I kept on trying and continually asked my riding-master as to when he thought I should be good enough to go riding in public, down Rotten Row. After a while, he was still not convinced, but didn't actually say no. "It's like this, you see, sir," he explained, "if you get hold of a quiet, steady horse, why, you won't come to no harm, but if you go out on a headstrong animal,

Mr Pulvertoft, why, you could get into a spot of trouble, sir."

They would have given me a horse at the school, but I knew most of the animals there, and none of them quite came up to my ideal of a quiet, steady horse, so I went to another stables nearby and asked if they had an animal that might suit me. The stable-master said that it just so happened that he had one which would suit me down to the ground.

I thought the horse looked perfect. He was a chestnut, of good proportions and had a sleek mane, but what reassured me was the calm look in his eye – he looked very noble for the small amount of money I was paying to hire him for the hour.

"You won't get a showier park 'orse than what he is, while at the same time very quiet," said his owner. "He's what you may call a kind 'orse, and very gentle."

I was powerfully drawn towards the horse. He seemed to know that he would have to be on his best behaviour if we rode in front of everyone, and he seemed to be very intelligent. With hardly a second thought, I booked him for the following afternoon.

Next day, I mounted at the stables feeling a little nervous and, at length, I found myself riding out into the London traffic on the back of the chestnut – whose name, by the way, was Brutus.

I shall never forget the pride and joy of having my steed under perfect control, as we threaded the maze of carriages with absolute security! I turned him into the park and clucked my tongue – he immediately broke into a canter and I was delighted to discover that it was not at all uncomfortable.

I said "Woa" and he stopped. When I asked him to trot, he trotted. I was so

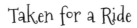

grateful, I could have kissed him!

Never before had I been upon a beast who was so easy to ride, who behaved so well. I could ride at last! Or at least, I could ride the horse I was on, and I decided that in future I would not ride any other.

We had crossed the Serpentine bridge and were just turning into Rotten Row when – and I know you won't believe this – I heard an unfamiliar voice addressing me with, "I say – you there!"

The moment afterwards, I realized it was coming from my horse! I am not ashamed to admit that I nearly fell off. Any rider would have, no matter how good. I was too busy trying to get my balance to reply straight away, so the horse spoke again. "I say," he inquired, in a rather cheeky tone, "do you think you can ride?"

I looked round in helpless bewilderment, at the shimmering Serpentine and the gleaming white houses in Park Lane, at the cocoa-coloured Rotten Row and the flash of distant carriage-wheels in the sunlight…

Everything looked normal, as usual – and yet, there was I on the back of a horse that had just inquired whether I thought I could ride!

"I have had two dozen lessons at a riding-school," I said at last, trying to sound confident in my abilities.

"I should hardly have suspected it," was his brutal retort. "You are clearly one of the most hopeless cases I've ever met."

I was deeply hurt. "I – I thought we were
getting on so nicely together," I faltered.
All he said in reply was, "Did you?"
"Do you know," I began, trying
to be friendly, "I have never

ridden a horse that talked before."

"You are enough to make any horse talk," he answered, "but I suppose I am an exception to the rule."

"I think you must be," said I. "And as you are obviously a very special horse, I understand that I made a dreadful mistake in riding you and, if you have the goodness to stand still, I will get off at once."

"Not so fast," said he. "I want to know something more about you first… I should say now that you were a man with plenty of oats."

"Well, I am reasonably well off," I fibbed. How I wished I was!

"I have long been looking out for an owner who would not overwork me," said the horse. "I want you to buy me."

"No," I gasped in shock, "and after you've been so rude about my riding, I'm surprised that you should even suggest such a thing."

"Oh, I will just have to put up with your bad riding," snorted the horse.

"You must excuse me," I blustered, "I don't want to buy a horse and, with your permission, I will spend the rest of the afternoon on foot."

"You will do nothing of the sort," said the horse.

"If you won't stop and let me get off properly," I said with distinct firmness, "I shall roll off onto the ground."

"I will run off with you first," the horse

replied. "You must see that you are in my power. Come, will you buy me, or shall I bolt away with you? I hate people who can't make up their mind!"

I had an idea. "Buy!" I said. "If you take me back, I will arrange it at once."

Needless to say, my plan was to get safely off his back, after which, nothing was going to make me buy him.

But, as we were heading back to the stables, the horse said thoughtfully, "I think it will be better if you make your offer to my owner before you dismount."

I was too vexed to speak – this clever animal had outwitted me!

And then we clattered into the stable yard. The stable-master cast his eyes up at the clock and said, "Why, you are home early, sir. You didn't find the 'orse too much for you, did you?"

He had no idea of the truth!

"Oh, dear no," I protested, "he carried me admirably – admirably!" I tried to slip off, but Brutus instantly jogged my memory and gave a little buck. Then he quickly

backed into the centre of the yard, stamping obstinately.

"I like him so much," I called out, as I clung to the saddle, "that I want to know if you would possibly sell him to me."

Here Brutus became calm and attentive.

"You step into my office here, sir," said the stable-master, "and we'll talk it over."

Of course, I should have been only too willing to get off, but the suspicious animal would not hear of it – he began to turn round and round immediately.

"Let us settle it now – here," I said, gripping on anxiously, "I can't wait."

The stable-master grinned at my urgency. "Well, we won't haggle, sir. Why don't we call it an even hundred."

I had no choice – I had to call it a hundred. I took him.

The Good Luck Horse

An ancient Chinese folk tale

This story was first written down over 2000 years ago,
by a prince called Liu An, in a book called The Huainanzi.

ONCE UPON A TIME in ancient China,
there was an old man who lived near
the northern border of the country. He was
very poor and struggled to make a living as
a farmer. But he was also very wise and
was well known for having a mysterious

skill – he could raise extremely fast, brave, intelligent horses.

One morning, the old man woke up to find that his favourite horse had broken out of its stall in the night and run away. He searched high and low, but could find no sign of where the stallion had gone.

The bad news spread like wildfire throughout the village, and the old man's neighbours came to see him to say how sorry they were. They expected to find the old man very downcast and upset, but to their amazement, he seemed contented. The neighbours came to comfort the old man but instead he had to reassure them!

"Do not worry yourselves," the old man told everyone. "This seems like bad luck, but it might turn out to be a blessing — you never know." The neighbours went away feeling very surprised indeed.

So the old man got on with his life quietly, without moaning once about the loss of his horse. Days, then weeks, then months went by until one day something wonderful happened.

The old farmer was out tilling his fields early in the morning when he saw an astonishing sight — his beloved stallion was approaching from the distance. And he wasn't alone, he was bringing with him a beautiful mare!

The old man gazed in disbelief for a few minutes, then he ran as fast as his aged legs could carry him to welcome back the

INTO THE SADDLE

stallion and his new companion, and lead
them safely home.

Once again, his neighbours soon came
gathering to share his happiness and
congratulate him. And again, they were
amazed by the old man's response. Instead
of finding him overjoyed and celebrating,

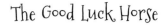

The Good Luck Horse

he was as calm and peaceful as before.

"Don't get so excited," the old man told everyone. "This seems like good luck, but it might turn out to be bad thing – you just never know."

The neighbours went away mumbling to themselves, shaking their heads in great confusion.

Now the old man had just one son, and he loved him very much. This son was an excellent horseman, like his father, and took it upon himself to break in and ride the newly arrived mare. As the weeks went by, the son taught the fine, wild horse to trust him, until the mare let him ride her wherever he wanted to go.

But one day, disaster struck! The mare

leaped a hedge and landed awkwardly, and the son fell off and broke both legs.

The old man's son had to spend several months lying in bed in pain before his legs were healed. Eventually, he was able to stand again, but his legs were not as they had been before. From then on, the son could only walk with the help of sticks. Yet the old man would not allow him to grumble. "My son," he said, "this might turn out to be a blessing – you never know."

And the son did his best to be brave and bear his suffering quietly, realizing that his father was a very wise man.

A year later, the terrible news came that a foreign army was attacking the northern border of China. All able-bodied young men were ordered to join the army and fight the invaders.

The old man's son saw all the young men from the village go off to fight – and most did not return. However, as he was injured, he was spared. He stayed at home with his father and their horses, and they lived many more happy years together.

Taming the Colt

From *Little Men* by Louisa M Alcott

Jo Bhaer and her husband run Plumfield School for mischievous boys. They encourage the students to develop an interest to help them become responsible young people. In this extract, a fourteen-year-old orphan called Dan finds an exciting pursuit…

A **FINE YOUNG HORSE** of Mr Laurie's was kept at Plumfield that summer, running loose in a large pasture across the brook. The boys were all interested in the handsome, spirited creature, affectionately known as Prince Charlie. For a time they

were fond of watching him gallop and frisk
with his plumey tail flying and his
handsome head in the air. But they soon
got tired of it and left the horse to himself.
All but Dan – he never tired of looking at
Charlie, and seldom failed to visit him each
day with a lump of sugar, a bit of bread or
an apple to make him feel welcome.

Charlie was grateful, accepted his
friendship, and the two loved one another.
In whatever part of the wide field he might
be, Charlie always came at full speed when
Dan whistled at the fence bars, and the boy
was never happier than when the beautiful
creature put its head on his shoulder,
looking up at him with fine eyes full of
intelligent affection.

INTO THE SADDLE

"We understand one another, don't we, old fellow?" Dan would say, proud of the horse's confidence. He was so protective of their friendship that he never asked anyone to accompany him on these daily visits.

Mr Laurie came now and then to see how Charlie got on. One day, he spoke of having him broken-in in the autumn.

"He won't need much taming, he is so gentle and fine-tempered. I shall come out and try him with a saddle myself some day," Mr Laurie said.

"He lets me put a halter on him, but I don't believe he will bear a saddle even if you put it on," answered Dan.

"I shall coax him to bear it and I won't mind a few tumbles at first. He has never been harshly treated, so I don't think he will be too frightened."

"I wonder what he would do," said Dan to himself, as Mr Laurie went away.

A daring fancy to try the experiment took possession of the boy as he sat on the topmost rail with the glossy back temptingly near him.

Never thinking of danger, Dan quickly and quietly took his seat. He did not keep it long, however, for with an astonished snort, Charlie reared straight up and threw Dan onto

the ground. The fall did not hurt him, for the turf was soft and he jumped up, saying, with a laugh,

"I did it anyway! Come here, you rascal, and I'll try it again."

But Charlie refused to approach and Dan left him with his mind made up to get him in the end.

Next time, Dan took a halter and after putting it on the horse, played with Charlie for a while, leading him to and fro, and putting him through various antics till he was a little tired. Then Dan sat on the wall and gave Charlie some bread, waiting for a good chance to grab the halter and slip on to his back. Charlie tried the old trick, but Dan held on. Charlie was amazed and,

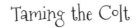

after prancing for a minute, set off at a gallop – away went Dan, heels over head, and he landed on the ground. He lay still, collecting his wits, while Charlie tore round the field, tossing his head with satisfaction.

Presently it seemed to occur to the horse that something was wrong with Dan and he went to see what the matter was. Dan let him sniff about, then looked up at him, saying, "You think you have won, but you are mistaken, old boy, and I'll ride you yet – just see if I don't."

Dan tried no more that day, but soon after attempted a new method. He strapped a folded blanket on Charlie's back and then let him race, and rear, and roll, and fume as much as he liked.

INTO THE SADDLE

After a few times Charlie calmed down and, in a few days, he permitted Dan to mount him. Dan patted and praised him, and took a short turn every day. He fell off frequently, but kept trying again in spite of that. He longed to try a saddle and bridle, but dared not tell anyone what he had done. However, unbeknown to him, the school caretaker, Silas, had seen him and put in a good word for him.

"Dan has been breaking the colt in, sir," Silas told Mr Bhaer one night, chuckling.

"How do you know?" asked the astonished school master.

"Well, when Dan kept going off to the pasture and coming home black and blue, I thought that something must be going on.

So I crept up to the field and spied on him, and I saw him going through all manner of games with Charlie. He was thrown about and knocked around like a sack of grain, but the plucky boy kept on going."

"But, Silas, you should have stopped it — the boy might have been killed," said

Mr Bhaer, wondering what on earth the pupils might get up to next.

"The fact was, he was doing so well I couldn't bring myself to stop it," replied Silas. "But now I know he's hankerin' after a saddle, so I thought I'd tell you and maybe you'd let him try. Mr Laurie won't mind, and Charlie's all the better for it."

"We shall see," and off went Mr Bhaer to inquire into the matter.

Dan owned up at once, and was eager to show everyone how well he could ride the horse. He proudly proved that Silas was right by showing off his power over Charlie, for by much coaxing, many carrots and infinite staying power, he really had succeeded in riding the colt with a halter and blanket. Mr Laurie was very much amused and well pleased with Dan's courage, determination and skill.

He set about Charlie's education at once and, thanks to Dan, the horse took kindly to the saddle and bridle. After Mr Laurie had trained him a little, Dan was permitted to ride him, to the great envy and admiration of the other boys.

"Isn't he handsome?" said Dan one day as he dismounted and stood with his arm round Charlie's neck.

"Yes, and isn't he a much more useful and agreeable animal than the wild colt who spent his days racing about the field, jumping fences, and running away now and then?" asked Mrs Bhaer from the steps where she was watching.

"Of course he is. See he won't run away now, even if I don't hold him, and he comes to me the minute I whistle. I have tamed him well, haven't I?"

Dan looked both proud and pleased – as well he might, for, in spite of their struggles together, Charlie loved him even better than his master.

"I am taming a colt too, and I think I shall succeed as well as you if I am as patient and persevering," said Mrs Jo, smiling significantly at Dan.

And Dan understood she meant him! Mrs Jo had been taming a colt of her own the whole time.

"We won't jump over the fence and run

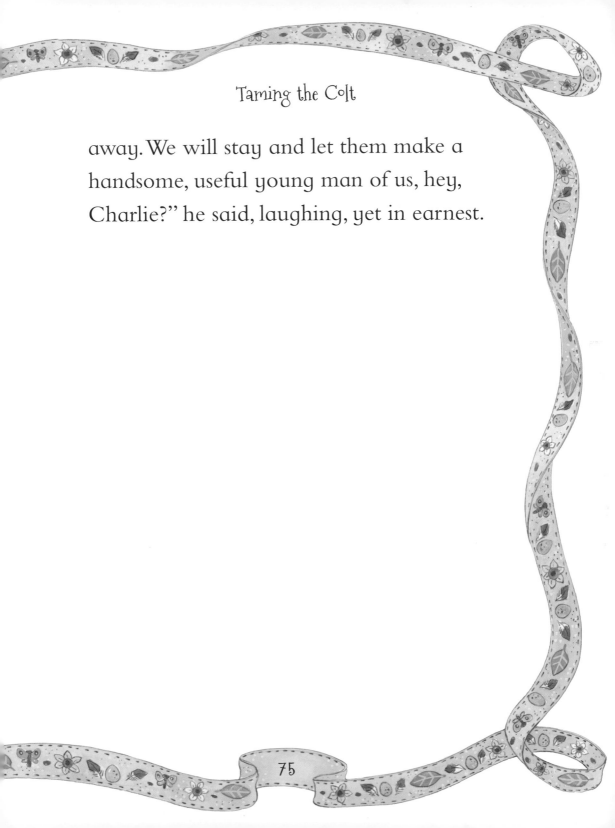

away. We will stay and let them make a handsome, useful young man of us, hey, Charlie?" he said, laughing, yet in earnest.

The Awakening
of the
Saw-horse

From *The Marvellous Land of Oz* by L Frank Baum

*In this extract, a young boy called Tip from the
Land of Oz escapes from a witch. He takes with him
a pumpkin-headed scarecrow called Jack, and a
magic powder that brings objects to life.*

TIP LED JACK, the pumpkin-headed
scarecrow, along the path without
stopping an instant. They could not go very
fast, but they walked steadily, and by the
time the moon sank away and the sun

peeped over the hills they had travelled so great a distance that the boy had no reason to fear pursuit from the old witch, Mombi. Moreover, he had turned first into one path, and then into another, so that it would prove very difficult to guess which way they had gone, or where to seek them.

Eventually, they came to the edge of a wood. Fairly satisfied that he had escaped – for a time, at least – Tip sat down to rest upon an old saw-horse that some woodcutter had left there.

"What is that thing you are sitting on?" asked the Pumpkinhead.

"Oh, this is a horse," replied the boy, carelessly.

"What is a horse?" demanded Jack.

"A horse? Why, there are two kinds of horses," returned Tip, slightly puzzled about how to explain. "One kind of horse is alive, has four legs and a head and a tail. And people ride upon its back."

"I understand," said Jack, cheerfully, "That's the kind of horse you are now sitting on."

"No, it isn't," answered Tip, promptly.

"Why not? That one has four legs, and a head, and a tail." Tip looked at the saw-horse more carefully, and found that the Pumpkinhead was right.

The body had been formed from a tree trunk, and a branch had been left sticking out at one end that looked very much like a tail. In the other end were two big knots

that resembled eyes, and a place had been
chopped away that might easily be
mistaken for the
horse's mouth.

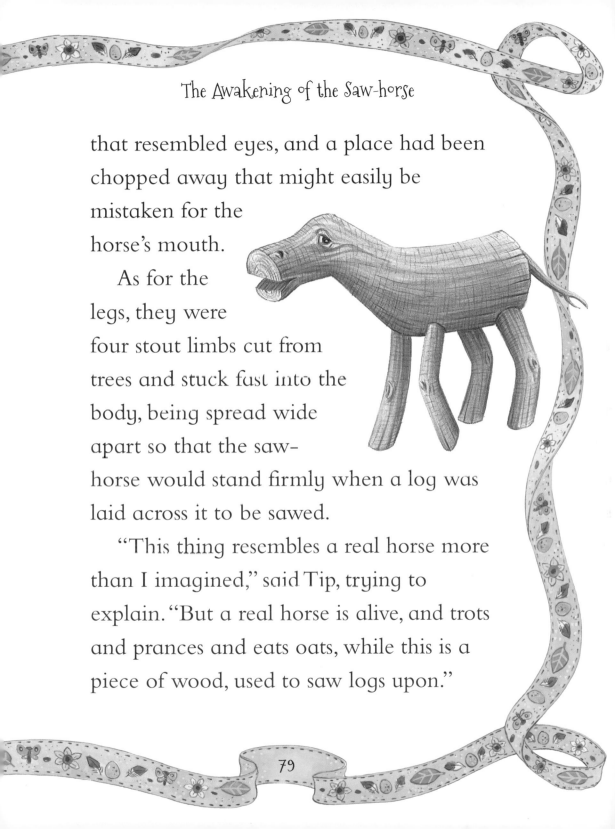

As for the
legs, they were
four stout limbs cut from
trees and stuck fast into the
body, being spread wide
apart so that the saw-
horse would stand firmly when a log was
laid across it to be sawed.

"This thing resembles a real horse more
than I imagined," said Tip, trying to
explain. "But a real horse is alive, and trots
and prances and eats oats, while this is a
piece of wood, used to saw logs upon."

"If it were alive, wouldn't it trot, and prance, and eat oats?" inquired the Pumpkinhead.

"It would trot and prance, perhaps, but it wouldn't eat oats," replied the boy, laughing at the idea. "And of course it can't ever be alive, because it is made of wood."

"So am I," answered the man.

Tip looked at him in surprise.

"Why, so you are!" he exclaimed. "And the magic powder that brought you to life is here in my pocket."

He brought out the pepper-box and eyed it curiously.

"I wonder," said he, musingly, "if it would bring the saw-horse to life."

"If it would," returned Jack calmly, for

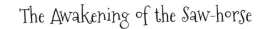

nothing seemed to surprise him, "I could ride on its back, and that would save my joints from wearing out."

"I'll try it!" cried the boy, jumping up. "But I wonder if I can remember the words old Mombi said, and the way she held her hands up."

He thought it over for a minute. He believed he could repeat exactly what she had said and done.

So he began by sprinkling some of the magic Powder of Life from the pepper-box upon the body of the saw-horse. Then he lifted his left hand, with the little finger pointing upwards, and said, "Weaugh!"

"What does that mean?" asked Jack.

"I don't know," answered Tip. Then he

lifted his right hand, with the thumb pointing upwards and said, "Teaugh!"

"What does that mean?" inquired Jack.

"It means you must keep quiet!" replied the boy, provoked at being interrupted at so important a moment.

"How fast I am learning!" remarked the Pumpkinhead, with his eternal smile.

Tip now lifted both hands above his head, with all the fingers and thumbs spread out, and cried in a loud voice, "Peaugh!"

Immediately the saw-horse moved, stretched its legs, yawned with its chopped-out mouth, and shook a few grains of the powder off its back. The rest of the powder seemed to have vanished into the body of the saw-horse.

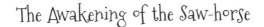

"Good!" called Jack, while the boy looked on in astonishment. "You are a very clever sorcerer!"

The saw-horse, finding himself alive, seemed even more astonished than Tip. He rolled his knotty eyes from side to side, taking a first view of the world in which he had now so important an existence. Then he tried to look at himself, but his neck was rigid so that in the attempt to see his body he kept circling around and around, without catching even a glimpse of it.

His legs were stiff and awkward, so when he tried to move, he bumped against Jack Pumpkinhead and sent him tumbling upon the moss that lined the roadside. Tip became alarmed at this accident, as well as at the persistence of the saw-horse in prancing around in a circle, so he called out, "Whoa! Whoa, there!"

The saw-horse paid no attention to this command and brought one of his wooden legs down upon Tip's foot so forcibly that the boy danced away in pain to a safer distance, from where he again yelled, "Whoa! Whoa, I say!"

Jack had now managed to raise himself to a sitting position and he looked at the saw-horse with much interest.

"I don't believe the animal can hear you," he remarked.

"I shout loud enough, don't I?" answered Tip, angrily.

"Yes, but the horse has no ears," said the

smiling Pumpkinhead.

"Sure enough!" exclaimed Tip, noting the fact for the first time. "How, then, am I going to stop him?"

But at that instant the saw-horse stopped himself, having concluded it was impossible to see his own body. He saw Tip, however, and came close to the boy to observe him more fully.

It was really comical to see the creature walk, for it moved the legs on its right side together, and those on its left side together, as a pacing horse does, and that made its body rock sidewise, like a cradle.

Tip patted it upon the head, and said "Good boy! Good boy!" in a coaxing tone, and the saw-horse pranced away to

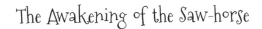

examine with its bulging eyes the form of Jack Pumpkinhead.

"Why don't you make him some ears?" asked Jack. "Then you can tell him what to do and he will hear you."

"That's a splendid idea!" said Tip. So Tip got out his knife and fashioned some ears out of the bark of a small tree.

The Pumpkinhead went to the horse and held its head while the boy made two holes in it with his knife and inserted the ears.

"They make him look very handsome," said Jack, admiringly.

But those words, spoken close to the saw-horse and being the first sounds he had ever heard, so startled the animal that he made a bound forwards and tumbled Tip on one side and Jack on the other. Then he continued to rush forwards as if frightened by the clatter of his own footsteps.

"Whoa!" shouted Tip, picking himself up. "Whoa, you idiot, whoa!"

The saw-horse would probably have paid no attention to this, but just then it stepped a leg into a hole and stumbled head-over-heels to the ground, where it lay upon its back, frantically waving its four legs in the air.

Tip ran up to it.

"Why didn't you stop when I yelled?" he exclaimed.

"Does 'whoa' mean to stop?" asked the saw-horse, in a surprised voice, as it rolled its eyes upwards to look at the boy.

"Of course it does," answered Tip.

"What am I doing here, anyway?" asked the horse in amazement.

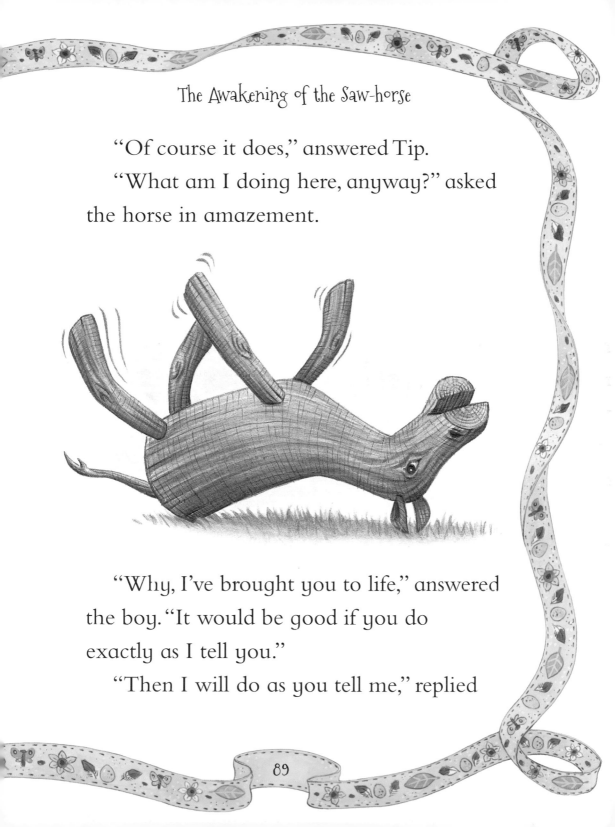

"Why, I've brought you to life," answered the boy. "It would be good if you do exactly as I tell you."

"Then I will do as you tell me," replied

the saw-horse, humbly. "But what happened to me, a moment ago? I don't seem to be the right way up now."

"You're upside down," explained Tip. "Just keep those legs still a minute and I'll set you the right way up."

The saw-horse now became quiet and held its legs rigid, so that Tip, after several efforts, was able to roll him over and set him upright once more.

"Ah, I seem all right now," said the strange animal, with a sigh.

"One of your ears is broken," Tip announced, after a careful examination. "I'll have to make a new one."

Then he led the saw-horse back to where Jack was vainly struggling to regain his feet and, after assisting him, Tip whittled out a new ear and fastened it to the horse's head securely.

"Now," said he, addressing his steed, "you must pay close attention to what I'm going to tell you. 'Whoa!' means to stop, 'Get-up!' means to walk forwards, and last of all, 'Trot!' means to go as fast as you can. Do you understand?"

"I believe I do," returned the horse.

"Very good. We are all going on a journey to the Emerald City, to see His Majesty. Now, Jack Pumpkinhead is going to ride on your back, so he won't wear out his joints."

"I don't mind," said the saw-horse.

Tip helped Jack get upon the saw-horse.

"Hold on tight," he cautioned.

So Jack held on tight and Tip said to the horse, "Get up."

The obedient creature at once walked forwards, rocking from side to side as he raised his feet from the ground.

Tip walked beside the saw-horse, quite content with this addition to their party.

After journeying on for some distance the narrow path they were following turned into a broad roadway, paved with yellow brick.

By the side of the road Tip noticed a sign-post that read:

EMERALD CITY

NINE MILES

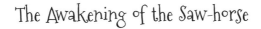

But it was now growing dark, so he decided to camp for the night by the roadside and to resume the journey next morning by daybreak.

Tip led the saw-horse to a grassy mound upon which grew several bushy trees, and carefully helped the Pumpkinhead to dismount safely.

"I think I'll lay you upon the ground, overnight," said the boy. "You will be safer that way."

"How about me?" asked the saw-horse.

"It won't hurt you to stand," replied Tip, "and, as you can't sleep, you may as well watch out and see that no one comes near to disturb us."

Then the boy stretched himself upon the

grass beside the Pumpkinhead and, watched over by the saw-horse, soon fell into a deep and peaceful sleep.

The Pony Rider Boys

From *The Pony Rider Boys in the Rockies*
by Frank Gee Patchin

Frank Gee Patchin wrote a series of twelve books called The Pony
Rider Boys. *Each story is set in America around one hundred
years ago. In this extract the four young lads decide to spend their
summer holidays in the saddle, exploring the beautiful wild
countryside of the Rocky Mountains in search of adventure.*

"OH, LET ME HAVE A GO! Let me ride
him for two minutes, please Walter."
Walter Perkins brought his pony to a
slow stop and glanced down hesitatingly
into the pleading blue eyes of the freckle-
faced boy at his side.

INTO THE SADDLE

"Please! I'll only ride him up to the end of the block and back, and I won't go fast, either. Let me show you how I can ride him," urged Tad Butler, with a note of insistence in his voice.

"If I thought you wouldn't fall off…"

"I fall off?" sniffed Tad, contemptuously. "I'd like to see the pony that could bounce me off his back. Huh! I know how to ride better than that. Say, Chunky, remember the time when the men from Texas brought those ponies here to sell?"

Chunky – the third boy of the group, whose real name was Stacy Brown – nodded vigorously.

"And didn't I ride a bronco that had only worn a saddle once?"

"He did," endorsed Chunky. "And he rode the pony three times around the baseball field, too. That bronco's back was humped up like a mad cat's all the way around. Course Tad can ride. Wish I could ride half as well as he does. You needn't be afraid, Walter."

Reassured by Chunky's praise, Walter dropped the bridle rein over the neck of his handsome new pony and slid slowly to the ground.

"All right, Tad. Jump up! But don't hold him too tightly. He doesn't like it and, besides, he has been trained to run when you tighten up on the rein and Father would not like it if we were to race him."

"I'll be careful."

INTO THE SADDLE

Tad Butler needed no second invitation to try out his companion's pony. With the agility of a cowboy, he leaped into the saddle without so much as touching a foot to the stirrup. In another second, with a slight pressure on the rein, he had wheeled the animal sharply on its haunches and was jogging off at an easy gallop. Yet, true to his promise, the boy made no effort to increase the speed of his mount. Nor did he go too far. Instead, he circled and came galloping back, one hand resting lightly on the rein, the other swinging easily at his side.

The soft breeze fanned bright colour into the face of seventeen-year-old Thaddeus Butler and his deep blue eyes glowed with excitement and pleasure, for, to him, there

was no happiness so great as that to be
found on the back of a swift-moving pony.

Tad had been born and brought up in
the little village of Chillicothe, Missouri,
same as Walter. Though Walter was the son
of a rich banker and Tad was poor, they
had been great friends since they were little.

Walter was a delicate boy and it was his

frail physical condition that had brought about the gift of the pony. The family doctor had advised it in order that the boy might have more outdoor air and, on this May morning, Walter had brought the pony out to show to his admiring friends.

"Tad's a good rider, isn't he?" breathed Chunky. Chunky was the son of a merchant in a small town in Massachusetts and had been visiting an uncle in Chillicothe for nearly a year.

"Yes, he does know how to ride," agreed Walter. "And, by the way, Father is going to get a horse for Professor Zepplin, my tutor, then we are going off on long rides every day, after my lessons are done. The doctor says it will be good for me. Fine to have a doctor like that, isn't it?"

"Great! Wish I could go along."

"Why don't you?" asked Walter, turning quickly to his companion. "That would be just the idea. What great times we could have, riding off into the open country! And we could go on exploring expeditions, too and make believe we were cowboys and all that sort of thing… And say! I'll tell you what," added the boy eagerly, "Tad, you and I will form ourselves into a club. Now, wouldn't that be great?"

"That would be fine!" glowed Chunky. "But what kind of a club? They don't have horses in clubs."

"We shall, in this one. That is, we shall be the club and the ponies will be our

club-house. When we are on our ponies'
backs we shall be in our club-house. Maybe
we can get Ned Rector to join us. He
knows how to ride – why, he rides almost
as well as Tad."

Chunky nodded thoughtfully.

"What shall we call it? We must have
some kind of a name for the club."

"I hadn't thought of that," said Walter.
"But here comes Tad back. Suppose we ask
him? He'll know just what we should call
call the club."

Tad reigned in alongside of them and
pulled the pony up sharply, patting its sleek
neck approvingly, loath to dismount.

"It's great, fellows. I wish I had a pony
just like this one. He's a great animal."

"I wish I had one too," echoed Chunky.

"Why, you don't have to touch the reins at all." said Tad. "I could ride him without just as well as with them. All you have to do is to press your knee against his side and he will turn, just as if you were pulling on the rein. He's a trained pony, Walter. Did you know that?"

"That's what the man said when Father bought him. Jo-Jo can walk on his hind legs, too. But Father said I mustn't try to make him do any tricks, for he fears I might get hurt."

"He wouldn't hurt a baby!" objected Tad in the little animal's defence. "I'll show you – I won't hurt him, don't be afraid," he exclaimed leaping to the ground, taking the rein over the animal's head and holding it at arm's length. "If he knows how to stand up I can make him do it. I've seen them do it in the circus."

Tad coaxed the horse by patting it gently on the side of the head, to which the intelligent animal responded by brushing his cheek softly with its nose.

"See, he knows a thing or two," cried Tad. "Now, watch me!"

Standing off a few feet, the boy tapped the animal very gently under the chin.

"Up, Jo-Jo! Up!" he urged, insistently. At first, Jo-Jo only swished his tail rebelliously, shaking his head until the bit rattled between his teeth.

But Tad wouldn't give up and he

persisted, gently yet firmly. Jo-Jo meanwhile pawed the dirt up into a cloud of dust that settled over the boys, finally causing a chorus of sneezes, until Tad felt sure he observed a twinkle of amusement in the eyes of the knowing little animal.

"Up, Jo-Jo!" he commanded almost sternly. The pony, recognizing the voice of a

master, hesitated no longer. Half folding his slender forelegs back, Jo-Jo rose slowly up.

Walter Perkins and Stacy Brown broke into a cheer. But Tad, never for an instant removing his gaze from Jo-Jo, held up a warning hand, leaned slightly forwards and fixed the pony with impelling eyes.

Then Tad backed away slowly. To the amazement of the others, Jo-Jo, balancing himself beautifully on his hind legs, followed his new-found master in short steps.

"Beautiful," breathed Walter and Chunky in chorus.

"He's amazing," added Chunky.

"How'd you do it, Tad?"

Before replying, the boy motioned to the pony that his task was done. Jo-Jo dropped quickly on all fours and, walking up to Tad, rubbed his nose affectionately against the lad's cheek once more.

"Good boy," soothed Tad, returning the caress with a stroke, his eyes were swimming with happiness.

But as Tad stepped back Jo-Jo insistently followed, alternately pushing his nose against the boy's face and tugging at his shirt. Jo-Jo was after something!

"Hey, got any sugar, Walter?" Tad asked, with a wide grin.

Walter quickly thrust a hand into a trouser pocket, and brought up a handful of sugar lumps that were far from being their natural colour.

Tad grabbed them and an instant later

Jo-Jo's quivering upper lip had closed greedily over the handful of sweets, and they were gone in an instant.

"That's what the little rascal wanted," breathed Tad with a pleased smile. "I could teach that pony to do most anything but talk, fellows."

"We were talking about setting up a club," spoke up Walter.

"Club? What kind of a club?" asked Tad absent-mindedly.

"Oh, just some sort of a riding club. But we can't just decide on the name. We had an idea that, perhaps, you might be able to think of a good title for it. What do you think, Tad?"

"I don't know. What about... The Pony

Rider Boys," suggested Tad.

And he walked over to the pony and laid his cheek against its nose, which he patted softly.

11o

NOBLE STEEDS

The White Horse

By E Nesbit

*Edith Nesbit lived in the English county of Kent
for around twenty years. The symbol for Kent has been a
white horse for over one thousand years. It is often referred
to as Invicta, which means unbeaten.*

ONCE UPON A TIME, there lived a simple
woodcutter's son called Diggory. When a
distant uncle sent Diggory the present of
a horse, he said goodbye to his father and
set out to seek his fortune. He christened the
horse 'Invicta'. It was white, with a red

saddle and bridle fit for a king, and all the village turned out to see him go.

Diggory rode to the windmill at the edge of the village, then stopped. For the miller's daughter, Joyce, came running up to him. "Take me with you," the pretty girl begged, earnestly. "I can ride behind you on your big horse."

But Diggory said, "No. Why, girls can't go to seek their fortunes. You'd only be in my way! Wish me luck."

So he rode on and she watched him go, her eyes brimming with tears.

Diggory rode on, and on. He rode through the dewy evening, and through the cool black night, and into the fresh-scented dawn. And when it was morning, Diggory felt very thin and empty, and he remembered that he had eaten nothing since dinner-time yesterday.

He rode on and on, and after a time came to a red brick wall, very strong and stout. Invicta was tall, so by standing up in his stirrups, Diggory could see over it. On the other side was an orchard of apple trees, all heavy with red and green fruits.

Diggory stood up on the broad saddle and jumped! In the next moment, he had hauled himself over the wall and dropped down into the orchard. For he was so hungry, he had made up his mind to take some apples.

Diggory climbed the tree with the fattest, rosiest apples. He had just settled himself

astride a
convenient
bough when
he heard a voice say,
"Hi! You up there!"
Looking down,
he saw an old man
looking up spitefully.
"Apple-stealing's punished severely in
these parts," he stated, narrowing his eyes.
"Besides, did you know that this is an
enchanted orchard? You can't just go away
as freely as you came in. Why, you can't
even get out of that tree…"

To Diggory's horror, he discovered that
the old man was right. He could move all
about the tree from branch to branch – but

suddenly he seemed to be upside down. If
he jumped off, he would fall up into the sky
– and keep falling upwards forever… So he
held tight and looked at the old man. And
Diggory thought that he looked nastier
than ever.

Then the old man said, "Look here,
throw me down those ten big apples so I
can catch them," he pointed to some apples
nearest the top of the tree, "and I'll let you
go out by the Apple Door that no one but
me has the key to."

"Why don't you pick them yourself?"
Diggory asked.

"I'm too old, you know very well
that old men don't climb trees. Come, is it
a bargain?"

"I don't know," said the boy, "there are lots of apples you can reach without climbing. Why do you want these so particularly?"

As he spoke, he picked one of the apples, threw it up and caught it. I say up, but it was down instead, because of the apple-tree being so very much enchanted.

"Oh, don't drop it!" the old man squeaked. "Throw it down to me, you nasty slack-baked, smock-frocked son of a speckled toad!"

Diggory's blood boiled at hearing his father called a toad.

"Take that!" cried he, aiming the apple at the old man's head. "I wish I could get out of this tree."

NOBLE STEEDS

The apple hit the old man's head and bounced onto the grass, and the moment that apple touched the ground Diggory found that he could get out of the tree if he liked, for he was now the proper way up, and so was the tree.

"So," he said, "are these wish-apples?"

"No, no, no!" shrieked the old man so earnestly that Diggory knew he was lying. "I've just disenchanted you, that's all, because I'm a nice kind old man really. They aren't wish-apples!"

"I wish you'd speak the truth," said Diggory, and with that he picked the second apple and threw it.

Then the old man couldn't help himself. "I am a wicked magician," he had to confess. "I never did anything useful with my magic. The apple trees in this orchard are people that I enchanted – I was going to do the same to you, too. Besides, there's only one way out of this place and I don't mean to show it you."

"It's a pity you're so wicked," said Diggory. "I wish you were good."

He threw down another apple and instantly the magician became so good that he could do nothing but sit down and cry to think how wicked he had been. Diggory was no longer afraid of him, so he gathered the ten apples that were left and put them inside his shirt, and came down the tree.

Then Diggory spent three wish-apples. First he used one to make the old man

happy, as well as good. Then Diggory threw
down another, and wished the apple trees to
be disenchanted – and they were.

The orchard was full of kings and
princesses, and swineherds and goosegirls,
and every kind of person you can or can't
think of.

The White Horse

The third apple showed Diggory the secret Apple Door. He went out through it and found his good white horse, who had been eating grass very happily all the time. So Invicta was not hungry, but Diggory was, and, in fact, he was so hungry that he had to use a wish-apple to get his supper.

After he had eaten, Diggory rode on anxiously, arranging what wishes he should have with the rest of the apples, but in the dusk he missed his way, plunged into a river and was nearly drowned, while poor white Invicta was quite carried away.

Having clambered onto the bank, Diggory took off his shirt to wring the water out and as he did so he said, "I wish I had my good white horse again."

And as he said it all the apples but one
tumbled out of his shirt onto the ground,
and he heard soft neighings and stampings
around him in the dark. When the moon
rose he saw that he had had his wish – his
good white horse was back again. But as
he had dropped eight apples, he had
his good white horse back eight times –
he had now eight good white horses, all
called Invicta.

"Well, eight horses are even better than
one!" he said, and when he had tethered the
horses he went to sleep, for he felt strangely
feeble and tired.

In the morning he woke with pains in
every limb. He thought it was probably a
cold from getting so wet in the river.

The White Horse

Diggory tied seven of the horses together and led them, riding on the eighth, home.

He knew the roads well enough, and yet they seemed different. They were much better roads to ride over, for one thing, and the hedges and trees were odd somehow. And the big wood near his father's house seemed very small as he looked down on it from the hill.

But when he got to the village he thought he must have gone mad, for in the few days that he had been away the village had grown bigger. There were eight shops and six pubs and many more people than there used to be, all in ugly clothes, and the windmill was gone! The people came crowding round him.

"What's become of the mill?" he asked, trembling all over.

The boys and girls and men and women stared, and a very old man stepped out of the crowd.

"It were pulled down," he said, "when I were a boy."

"And the woodcutter's cottage?"

"That were burned down a matter of fifty year ago. Were you a native of these parts, old man?"

There was a large shop-window just opposite and Diggory suddenly saw his reflection in it – an old, old, white-haired man on a white horse. He had a white beard, too.

He almost tumbled off Invicta. The

landlord of one of the pubs led him in to sit
by the fire in the bar and the eight horses
were put up in the stable.

The old man who had told him about
the mill came and sat by him, and poor old
Diggory asked questions about all the

people he knew and loved till he grew tired of hearing the answer, which was always the same, "Dead… dead… dead!"

Then he sat silent, and the people in the bar talked about his horses, and a young man said, "I wish I'd got just one of them. I'd set myself up in business, so I would."

"Young man," said Diggory, "you may take one, its name is Invicta."

The young man could hardly believe his ears. Diggory felt his heart warm to think that he had made someone else so happy. He actually felt younger. The very next morning he made up his mind to give away all the horses but one.

He led his horses away next day and gave away one in each village he passed through – and with every horse he gave away he felt happier and lighter. And when he had given away the fourth, his aches and pains went, and when he had given away the seventh his beard was gone.

"Now," he said to himself, "I will ride home and end my days in my own village."

So he turned his horse's head towards home, and he felt so much happier and fitter he could hardly believe that he was really an old, old man.

He rode on and when he reached the end of his village he stopped and rubbed his eyes, for there stood the windmill and there was Joyce, looking prettier than ever.

"Oh, Diggory," she cried, "you've come back. Will you take me with you now?"

"Have you got a looking-glass?" he said. "Run and fetch it."

She brought it quickly and he looked in it, and he saw he was not old any more!

"Will you take me with you?" said Joyce.

He stooped down and kissed her sweet, pretty face.

"Of course," said he.

And as they went along to his home he told her the story.

"Well," she said, "you've got one wish-apple left."

"Why, so I have," said he.

"We'll make that into the fortune you went out to find," clever Joyce said.

And Diggory carried Joyce on Invicta to his father's house.

The White Horse

"You're soon back, my son," said the woodcutter, laughing.

"Yes," said Diggory.

"Have you found your fortune?"

"Yes," said Diggory, "here she is!"

"Well, well!" the woodcutter said, laughing more than ever.

So they were married, and they used the last wish-apple to set themselves up on a little farm. Diggory, Joyce and the white horse worked hard on the farm, so that they all prospered and were very happy as long as ever they lived.

The Lightning Horse and the Prince of Persia

By James Baldwin

This is a retelling of a folktale from Persia (modern-day Iran). It was first written down by a poet called Ferdowsi, around one thousand years ago in the 'Shanameh', or 'Book of Kings', a mixture of Persian mythology and history dating back to the beginning of the world.

WHEN RUSTEM was still a young man, the news came that a vast army of enemies had come down from the north and were threatening to cross into Persia. Rustem begged his father, a prince, to let him lead a band of warriors against the invaders. These words pleased his father, who at once sent out a proclamation into all the provinces, commanding that on the first day of the Festival of Roses all the best horses should be brought to Zaboulistan so that Rustem could choose one of them to be his battle steed. The owner of the one that was selected would be rewarded with mountains of gold, but if anyone should hide a good horse, he would be punished without mercy.

On the appointed day, the most famous horse breeders from across all Persia had assembled their finest horses at Zaboulistan. Even more horses had been brought in by common folk. Everyone had brought the best that he had, and the world had never seen a nobler or more wonderful collection of steeds.

At an early hour in the morning, Prince Zal and young Rustem took up position outside the city gate in a covered pavilion. One by one the horses were led before them. All were swift and strong, and many had been bred especially for Rustem to use one day. But none of them satisfied the young prince.

After hours had passed, the very last horses were presented by some traders from Kabul. But Rustem's eyes moved from the steeds in front of him to another couple of horses further off.

"Whose is that mare over there?" asked

Rustem. "And whose is the colt that stays so close to her?"

"We do not know," answered the traders. "But they have followed us all the way from the Afghan valleys, and we have been unable to capture them. We have heard it said, however, that men call the colt Rakush, or Lightning, and that his mother will let no one touch him."

The colt was a beautiful animal. It gleamed like burnished gold, its chest and shoulders were like those of a lion, and its

eyes beamed with the fire of intelligence.
Snatching a noose from the hands of a
herdsman, Rustem ran quickly forwards
and threw it over the animal's head. Then
followed a terrible battle, not so much with
the colt as with its mother. But in the end
Rustem was the winner and the mare
cantered away, crestfallen, from the field.
With a great bound the young prince
leaped upon Rakush's back and the golden
steed bore him over the plains with the
speed of the wind.

Rustem raced back to the city gate.
"This is the horse that I choose," he told his
father. "Let us give the traders their reward."

"No," answered the men. "Have him
with our blessing and save the lands of Iran

– for, seated upon Rakush, no enemy will be able to stand before you."

Their words proved true. For Rustem and Rakush led an attack that beat back the invaders – which was only the first bold, brave feat of many. It would take an entire book to tell all the daring adventures of Rakush and his master – how they became so inseparable that their names were always spoken together, never one without the other, and how they became famous throughout the length and breadth of Iran.

For instance, the Shah of Persia was once captured by the King of Mazinderan. From his dungeon, he managed to write a note asking for help and smuggle it to Prince Zal in Zaboulistan. Prince Zal at once told his son to speed to the Shah's aid to rescue him.

So Rustem mounted Rakush and set out by the shortest road across the Great Salt Desert that lies toward Mazinderan, and such was the speed of Rakush that the two-day journey took them only twelve hours.

Late in the evening, Rustem lay down to rest, turning Rakush loose to graze. However, a fierce lion crept forwards to attack them. Rakush heard him coming and, before the lion could make a spring, leaped upon him, beat him down with his hoofs and stamped upon him. Rustem, awakened by the terrible noise, sprang to his feet, but his brave horse Rakush had already killed the lion.

At the first peep of dawn Rustem and

Rakush set off once more. All day long he rode over the barren wastes. The hot sun beat down pitilessly and the sand beneath them was like a burning oven. At length Rustem was so overcome by the heat and with thirst that he lost all hope and lay down in the sand to die.

But just then he chanced to see a fine sheep running nearby. "Surely," thought he, "there must be water not far away, or this animal could not be here." The hope gave him new courage and, remounting Rakush, he urged him forwards.

They didn't have to follow the sheep far, for it led them into a narrow green valley, through the middle of which ran a little brook. Man and beast drank their fill.

NOBLE STEEDS

When at length the sun had set and the
stars had risen, Rustem lay down to sleep
while Rakush quietly grazed. All was well
until near midnight, when a fierce dragon
that lived in the valley came out of his den.
It was astonished to see the horse feeding
and a man asleep not far away.

The dragon was just ready to destroy
them with his poisonous breath when
Rakush, seeing the danger, neighed
frantically to awaken his master.

Rustem sprang up quickly and seized his
sword. The dragon leaped upon Rustem
and wrapped itself about him, and would
surely have crushed him to death had not
Rakush come to the rescue. The horse used
his teeth to seize the dragon from behind

and, as it turned to defend itself, Rustem's arm was freed so that he could use his sword. With one mighty stroke he cut off the dragon's head, and the vile serpent of the desert was no more.

Then Rustem praised Rakush highly for his great courage. He carefully washed his gallant horse in the stream, and groomed Rakush until the break of day, and when the sun arose they set out on another day's journey across the burning sands.

Needless to say, Rustem and Rakush triumphed over every peril they met on their way, despite the dangers that befell them in the land of the magicians and in the country of darkness, where there was no light of sun or stars, and where they were guided by Rakush's instinct alone.

Eventually they arrived in Mazinderan and, after meeting innumerable dangers, delivered the Shah from his dungeon and returned him safely home.

In all the East there was no hero that could be likened unto Rustem, and never a horse that could in any way be compared with Rakush. Many years passed by – years of peace and years of war – and many Shahs sat upon the throne of Iran, but the real power was in the hands of Rustem of Zaboulistan.

And although he lived to a great age, and Rakush was so very, very old that he was no longer of the colour of rose-leaves, but white as the snow of winter, both of

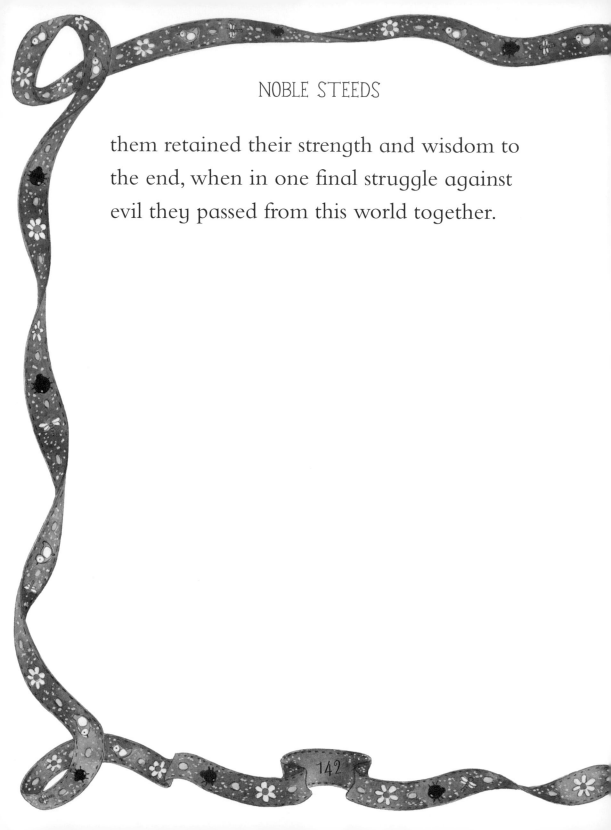

them retained their strength and wisdom to the end, when in one final struggle against evil they passed from this world together.

Soldier-boy

From *A Horse's Tale* by Mark Twain

*Buffalo Bill was the nickname of American soldier and bison hunter
William Frederick Cody, who lived through the last days of the
Wild West, from 1846 to 1917. He was awarded the Medal of
Honour for his services to the US army as a scout and later became
famous for organizing shows with cowboy themes, which he toured
around the United States, Europe and Great Britain.*

I AM BUFFALO BILL'S HORSE. I have spent
my life under his saddle – with him in it,
too, and he is two hundred pounds, without
his clothes, and there is no telling how much
he weighs when he is out on the warpath
and has his ammunition belted on.

He is young, over six feet, hasn't an

ounce of waste flesh, is straight, graceful, and nimble – quick as a cat. He has a handsome face and black hair dangling down on his shoulders and is beautiful to look at, and nobody is braver than he is, and nobody is stronger, except myself.

Yes, a person that doubts that he is fine to see should see him in his beaded buckskins, on my back and his rifle peeping above his shoulder, chasing an enemy, with me going like the wind and his hair streaming out behind him. Yes, he surely is a sight to look at then – and I'm part of it myself.

I am his favourite horse, out of dozens. I am not large but, big as he is, I have carried him thousands and thousands of miles on

scout duty for the army. There's not a
gorge, nor a pass, nor a valley, nor a fort,
nor a trading post, nor a buffalo-range in
the whole sweep of the Rocky Mountains
and the Great Plains that we don't know as
well as we know the bugle-calls. He is Chief
of Scouts to the Army of the Frontier, and it
makes us very important.

In such a position as I hold in the
military service one needs to be of good
family and be much better educated than
most. Well, everybody says that I am the
best-educated horse this side of the Atlantic,
and the best-mannered. It may be so, it is
not for me to say, modesty is the best policy,
I think.

Buffalo Bill taught me the most of what

Soldier-boy

I know, my mother taught me some, and then I taught myself the rest. Lay a row of moccasins before me and I can tell you which tribe it comes from just by looking at it – Pawnee, Sioux, Shoshone, Cheyenne, Blackfoot, and as many other tribes as you please… name them in horse-talk that is, and I could do it in American if I had the means to speak aloud.

I know some of the Indian signs – the signs they make with their hands and by signal-fires at night and columns of smoke by day. Buffalo Bill taught me how to drag wounded soldiers out of the line of fire with my teeth, and I've done it, too – at least I've dragged him out of the battle when he was wounded. And not just once, but twice.

NOBLE STEEDS

Yes, I know a lot of things. I remember bodies and faces and the way people walk, and if anyone ever shows me kindness I'll remember them forever.

I know the art of searching for a trail and I know the stale track from the fresh. I can keep a trail all by myself, with Buffalo Bill asleep in the saddle – just ask him and he will tell you so. Many a time, when he has ridden all night, he has said to me at dawn, "Take the watch, Boy, if the trail freshens, call me."

Then he goes to sleep. He knows he can trust me, because I have an excellent reputation and have never let him down.

Now, I'll tell you a bit about my background. My mother was all American – she was of the best blood of Kentucky, the bluest Blue-grass aristocracy, and very proud. She spent her military life as the Colonel of the Tenth Dragoons, and saw a great deal of distinguished service. I mean, she carried the Colonel, but it's all the same. After all, where would he be without his horse? He simply wouldn't arrive – it takes two to make a colonel of dragoons.

My mother was a fine dragoon horse, but she never got above that. She was strong enough for the scout service, and had the endurance too, but she couldn't quite come up to the speed required – a scout horse has to have steel in his muscle and lightning in his blood.

My father on the other hand was a bronco, as wild as they come. When Professor Marsh was out here hunting bones for Yale University he found skeletons of horses no bigger than a fox, bedded in the rocks, and he said they were ancestors of my father – two million years old!

Professor Marsh said those skeletons were fossils. So that makes me part blue grass and part fossil, if there is any older or better stock, I'd like to know about it.

And now we are back at Fort Paxton once more, after a forty-day scout, away up as far as the Big Horn river. Everything quiet. Crows and Blackfeet squabbling – as usual – but no outbreaks, and so the settlers are feeling fairly easy.

The Seventh Cavalry is still in garrison, here, as are the Ninth Dragoons, two artillery companies, and some infantry. They are all mighty glad to see me, including General Alison, the commandant.

The officers' ladies and children are very friendly. They call by to see me – and bring sugar with them. It was Tommy Drake and Fanny Marsh that remembered the sugar

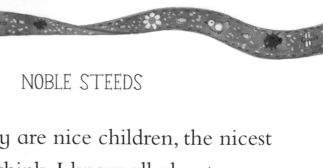

this time. They are nice children, the nicest at the post, I think. I know all about children, and they adore me. Buffalo Bill will tell you so himself.

The Naming of Black Beauty

From *Black Beauty* by Anna Sewell

In this extract from Black Beauty *the young horse is taken away
from the farm on which he was born. Bought by the wealthiest man
in a local village, Squire Gordon, he settles quite happily into life
on his country estate and is given a name at last…*

I LIVED FOR SOME YEARS with Squire
Gordon. Squire Gordon's park skirted the
village of Birtwick. It was entered by a
large iron gate, at which stood the first
lodge, and then you trotted along on a
smooth road between clumps of large old

trees, then there was another lodge and another gate, which brought you to the house and the gardens. Beyond this lay the paddock, the old orchard and the stables.

There was stabling for many horses and carriages. I was taken into a very roomy one, with four good stalls. A large swinging window opened into the yard, which made it pleasant and airy. The first stall was a large square one, shut behind with a wooden gate. The others were common stalls, good stalls, but not nearly so large.

Mine had a low rack for hay and a low manger for corn. It was called a loose box, because the horse that was put into it was not tied up, but left loose, to do as he liked.

The sides were low enough so that I

could see all that went on through the iron
rails that were at the top. The groom gave
me some very nice oats, he patted me, spoke
kindly, and then went away.

When I had eaten my corn I looked
round. In the stall next to mine stood a little
fat grey pony, with a thick mane and tail, a

very pretty head, and a pert little nose.

I put my head up to the iron rails at the top of my box, and said, "How do you do? What is your name?"

He held up his head, and said, "My name is Merrylegs. I am very handsome, I carry the young ladies on my back, and sometimes I take our mistress out in the ow carriage. They think a great deal of me. Are you going to live next door to me in the box?"

I said, "Yes."

"Well, then," he said, "I hope you are good-tempered, I do not like anyone next door who bites."

Just then a horse's head looked over from the stall beyond, the ears were laid back, and the eye looked rather ill-tempered. This was a tall chestnut mare, with a long handsome neck. She looked across to me and said, "So it is you who have turned me out of my box, it is a very strange thing for a colt like you to come and turn a lady out of her own home."

"I beg your pardon," I said, "I have turned no one out, the man who brought me put me here, and I had nothing to do with it, and as to my being a colt, I am turned four years old and am a grown-up horse. I never had words yet with horse or mare and it is my wish to live at peace."

"Well," she said, "we shall see."

I said no more.

In the afternoon, when she went out,

Merrylegs told me about it.

"The thing is this," said Merrylegs.
"Ginger has a bad habit of biting and
snapping – that is why they call her Ginger,

and when she was in the loose box
she used to snap very much. One day
she bit the groom's boy, James, in the arm
and made it bleed, and so Miss Flora and
Miss Jessie, who are very fond of me, were

afraid to come into the stable. They used to bring me nice things to eat, an apple or a carrot, or a piece of bread, but after Ginger stood in that box they dared not come, and I missed them very much indeed. I hope they will now come again, if you do not bite or snap."

I told him I never bit anything but grass, hay, and corn, and could not think what pleasure Ginger found in it.

"Well, I don't think she does find pleasure," says Merrylegs, "it is just a bad habit, she says no one was ever kind to her, and why should she not bite? Of course, it is a very bad habit, but I am sure, if all she says be true, she must have been very ill-used before she came here. John does all he can to please her, and James does all he can, and our master never uses a whip if a horse acts right, so I think she might be good-tempered here.

"You see," he said, with a wise look, "I am twelve years old, I know a great deal, and I can tell you there is not a better place for a horse all round the country than this. John is the best groom that ever was - he has been here fourteen years, and you never saw such a kind boy as James is, so it is all Ginger's own fault that she did not stay in that box."

The next day I was prepared for my master to ride. I remembered my mother's advice and I tried to do exactly what he wanted me to do.

The Naming of Black Beauty

I found that he was a very good rider and thoughtful for his horse too.

When he came home, Mrs Gordon was at the hall door as he rode up.

"Well, my dear," she said, "how do you like him?"

"He is exactly what John said," he replied, "a pleasanter creature I never wish to mount. What shall we call him?"

"What about Ebony?" said she, "For he is as black as ebony."

Squire Gordon thought for a moment, then declared, "No, not Ebony."

"What about Blackbird, like your uncle's old horse?"

"No, he is far more handsome than old Blackbird ever was."

"Well," she said, "he is really quite a beauty, and he has such a sweet, good-tempered face, and such a fine, intelligent eye – what do you say to calling him Black Beauty?"

"Black Beauty… Why, yes, I think that is

a very good name. If you like, it shall be his name," decided Squire Gordon.

And so it was.

The War Horse of Alexander

By Andrew Lang

Alexander the Great was a powerful military leader that lived over two thousand years ago. He led invading armies over Europe and into Asia to create one of the largest ever empires. His horse, Bucephalus, is almost as legendary, and has been described as a massive, black creature with a white star upon his enormous brow.

THERE ARE NOT NEARLY AS MANY stories about horses as there are about dogs and cats, yet almost every great general has had his favourite horse, who has gone with him through many campaigns and borne him safely in many battlefields.

The most famous horse who ever lived was perhaps one belonging to the ancient Macedonian king, Alexander the Great. His noble horse was called Bucephalus. This is how Alexander came by him…

When Alexander was just a boy, a trader presented Bucephalus to his father, King Philip of Macedon. The trader offered him for the very large sum of thirteen talents, which was the type of money used in Macedon. Beautiful though the horse looked, the king wisely refused to buy him before knowing what his character was like.

So King Philip ordered Bucephalus to be led into a neighbouring field and asked a groom to mount him. But it soon became apparent that the horse wouldn't let anyone come near him – when even the best and most experienced riders approached him, he reared up on his hind legs, and they were forced to back away.

The trader was told to take his horse away, for the king would have none of him. However the king's son, Alexander, stood by watching all that went on, and his heart went out to the beautiful creature.

He cried out to his father, "Stop! We are going to lose a good horse because no one has the skill to mount him!"

King Philip heard these words and agreed it was a terrible shame to let the horse be taken away. He thought to himself for a moment, then turned to his son and said, "Do

you think that you, who are young and haven't been riding long, can ride this horse better than older, expert riders?"

To which Alexander answered, "I know I can ride this horse better than any of them. Please let me try."

"But if you fail," said King Philip, "I will have lost a huge amount of money in paying for him!"

Alexander laughed out loud and said with glee, "I will give you the money then." And so it was settled.

So Alexander drew near to the horse and took him by the bridle, turning his face to the sun so that he might not be frightened by the movements of his own shadow, for the prince had noticed that it scared him greatly.

Then Alexander stroked the horse's head and led him forwards. The second the horse began to get uneasy, the prince suddenly leaped onto his back and took charge of him with firm hands upon the bridle.

As soon as Bucephalus gave up trying to throw his rider, and only pawed the ground Alexander shook the reins and, bidding him go, they flew away like lightning.

Taming Bucephalus was Alexander's first conquest. His father was delighted and said, "Macedonia is obviously too small a country for you – you should go out and conquer other, greater challenges. I know you are capable of great things."

So from that moment on, Bucephalus made it clear that he served Alexander and no one else. The horse would stand quietly while the royal saddle was put on him and the rich trappings of a king's steed were fastened on his head, but if any groom tried to mount him, back would go his ears and up would go his heels. None dared come near him.

Bucephalus bore Alexander through all his battles and even when wounded, as he once was at the taking of Thebes, would not suffer his master to mount another horse.

Together these two swam rivers, crossed mountains, conquered kingdoms and won lands in the heart of Asia, where no European army had gone before.

When, after ten years of adventures and victories, old Bucephalus died, Alexander was heartbroken. He gave his horse the most

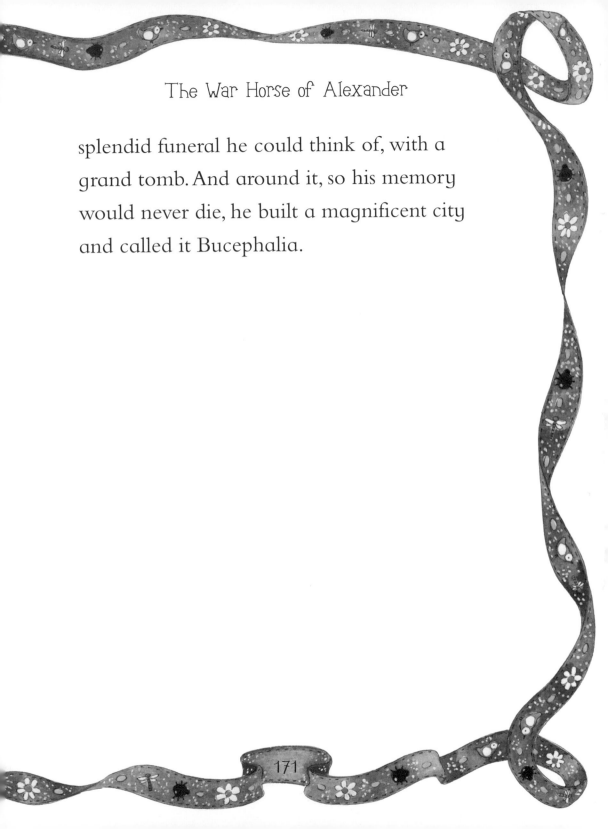

splendid funeral he could think of, with a grand tomb. And around it, so his memory would never die, he built a magnificent city and called it Bucephalia.

Old Gunpowder and the Ghost

From *The Legend of Sleepy Hollow* by Washington Irving

*This story is set over 200 years ago in North America.
At the beginning, a schoolteacher called Ichabod Crane arrives
in an area of quiet countryside inhabited by Dutch settlers.
He hopes to win the hand of Katrina Van Tassel, a wealthy
farmer's daughter, but so does another man, Brom Bones.*

ICHABOD SPENT AT LEAST an extra half
hour getting ready, dusting off his one and
only suit, and arranging his locks by a bit of
broken looking-glass that hung up in the
schoolhouse. He borrowed a horse from a

neighbouring farmer and set out like a gallant knight in quest of adventures.

In reality, the animal he rode was an old and tired plough-horse. It was bony, with a drooping neck, and a head like a hammer. The horse had a rusty mane and its tail was tangled and knotted. One eye had clouded over and was glassy and glaring, while the other had a mischievous gleam in it. However, in his day he must have had fire and courage, because his name was Gunpowder.

Ichabod was a suitable rider for such a steed. He rode with short stirrups, which brought his knees nearly up to the pommel of the saddle, and his sharp elbows stuck out like grasshoppers' knees. He carried his whip straight up in his hand, like a sceptre, and, as his horse jogged on, his arms flapped like a pair of wings. Such was the appearance of Ichabod and his steed as they shambled out of the gate.

It was a fine autumnal day. Ichabod and Gunpowder journeyed along the side of a range of hills that looked out upon the mighty Hudson river. The sun gradually dipped down in the west and it was towards evening that he arrived at the mansion of the Van Tassel family.

It was thronged with country folk and soon Ichabod found himself enjoying the charms of a genuine Dutch country tea-table, heaped up with delicious food.

Then came the dancing, and Ichabod

was overjoyed that Katrina Van Tassel agreed to be his partner. On the other hand, Brom Bones, sorely smitten with love and jealousy, sat brooding by himself in one corner, watching with a beady eye.

When the dance was at an end, Ichabod spoke to some older folks, who sat with Katrina's father, discussing old times and

drawing out long stories about the war. Each storyteller dressed up his tale with a few extra details and managed to make himself the hero of every exploit.

But all these war adventures were nothing to the ghost stories that soon followed. The neighbourhood was rich in such spooky tales, largely due to the closeness of a glade called Sleepy Hollow. Rumour said it was haunted. Many tales were told about a great tree where mourning cries and wailings were heard.

Some mention was made about a woman in white who was reported to haunt the dark glen at Raven Rock, and was often heard to shriek on winter nights before a storm. But most of the stories

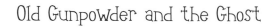

centred upon the favourite ghost of Sleepy Hollow, the Headless Horseman, who had been heard lately near an old churchyard.

Eventually the revel gradually broke up and the partygoers began to make their way home. Ichabod lingered to have a private talk with Katrina, fully convinced that he was now on the road to winning her hand. What they spoke about I do not know. However, it clearly did not go as well as he had hoped, for he left after a short time, looking rather upset.

He went straight to the stable and woke old Gunpowder rudely from the comfortable quarters in which he was sleeping, dreaming of corn and oats.

It was the very witching time of night

when Ichabod, heavy-hearted, pursued his travels homewards, along the sides of the lofty hills, which he had passed so cheerily in the afternoon. There were no signs of life except the melancholy chirp of a cricket, or the twang of a bullfrog.

The night grew darker and darker, the stars seemed to sink deeper in the sky, and driving clouds occasionally hid them from his sight. All the ghost stories he had heard now came crowding upon his thoughts.

His heart began to thump as he approached Sleepy Hollow and neared a bridge over a stream. Suddenly, something dark and towering rose up in the gloom at his side, like a gigantic monster.

With a scramble and a bound, it stood at

once in the middle of the
road, very close to Ichabod
and Gunpowder.

In the darkness, Ichabod
could make out what
looked like a huge rider,
mounted on a dark,
powerful horse.

He pressed Gunpowder forward in the
hope of a quick escape, but the dark
horseman and his steed kept pace with
every step.

Then, suddenly the clouds
parted and the moon shone
down. To Ichabod's
horror, he saw
that the

horseman was headless! And the head that should have rested on his shoulders was actually being carried upon his saddle!

Ichabod's terror rose to desperation. He rained a shower of kicks and blows upon Gunpowder and the horse dashed away, the ghostly horseman and his demon steed pelting after them. Gunpowder plunged headlong through Sleepy Hollow, going at such a pace that the girths of the saddle gave way, and it slid from under Ichabod and fell to the ground. The schoolteacher heard it trampled by the hooves of the ghost horse and rider in hot pursuit.

Now jolted along on his horse's backbone, Ichabod saw the walls of a church looming on the other side of the bridge. 'If I can only reach that,' he thought, 'I am safe.'

Just then he heard the steed panting and blowing close behind him, and even fancied that he felt his hot breath. Another kick in the ribs, and old Gunpowder thundered over the remaining planks and plunged into the churchyard on the other side.

Now Ichabod cast a look behind to see if his evil pursuer should vanish in a flash of fire and brimstone on reaching holy ground. But he saw the horseman rise in his stirrups and hurl his head at him! Ichabod tried to dodge it, but too late. It hit his own head with a tremendous crash and the dazed schoolteacher tumbled into the dust.

Next morning old Gunpowder was

found without his saddle, and with his
bridle under his feet, cropping the grass at
the gate of the farmer who owned him. And
at the churchyard entrance there lay a
smashed pumpkin. But there was no sign
of Ichabod...

Pegasus, the Winged Horse

By James Baldwin

Pegasus is one of the most famous horses of all time. According to the myths of ancient Greece, he was a son of the god of the ocean, Poseidon. There are many stories about the partnership between Pegasus and a hero called Bellerophon.

PEOPLE SAID THAT THE GODS sent him to the earth. But to this day nobody really knows anything about how Pegasus came to exist.

One day, full of energy and strength, he

came swooping down on to a main road
that runs towards the great city of Lycia.

Pegasus descended so softly and folded
his great wings so gently and set his feet
upon the ground so quietly, that a young
man who was walking along nearby didn't
even notice that Pegasus had arrived until
he had cantered right
up next to him.

The young
man was full of
admiration for
the beautiful
animal and
reached out his
hand to stroke
his soft nose —

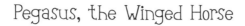

the horse turned away and flew off as quick
as an arrow.

The young man walked on, but the
horse returned and gambolled playfully
around him, sometimes trotting back and
forth, sometimes rising in the air and sailing
in circles round and round him. At last, the
young man coaxed the horse close enough
to leap onto his back, just in front of his
great grey wings.

By late in the afternoon, when they had
left the pleasant farmland around Lycia far
behind them, they landed at the border of a
wild, deserted region. An old man with a
long white beard and bright glittering eyes
met them and stopped to admire the
beautiful animal.

"Who are you, young man," he inquired, "and what are you doing with so handsome a steed here in this lonely place?"

"My name is Bellerophon," answered the young man, "and I am going by order of King Lobates to the country beyond the northern mountains, where I am going to try to slay a fire-breathing monster called the Chimaera, which lives there. I cannot tell you where this horse comes from or who he belongs to, for I do not know."

The old man was silent for a few moments, then said, "Do you see the white roof over there among the trees? Under it there is a shrine to the goddess Athena, of which I am the keeper. A few steps beyond it is my own humble cottage. If you will go in and lodge with me for the night, I may be able to tell you something about the task that you have undertaken."

Bellerophon was very glad to accept the old man's invitation, for the sun had already begun to dip below the western hills. The hut was small but clean and cosy. The kind host gave Bellerophon supper, made him comfortable, and then looked him straight in the eye and said, "Now tell me all about yourself and why you are going alone into the country of the Chimaera."

"My father," answered Bellerophon, "is King Glaucus of Corinth. I am brave and fond of hunting wild beasts, and am anxious to win fame by doing some daring deed. I heard that the people who live on the other side of the northern mountains are in great dread of a strange animal called the Chimaera that comes out of the caves and carries off their flocks, and sometimes their children too. I made up my mind to kill it. So I found the shortest road to the mountains and – here I am!"

Then the old man said, "I have heard of this Chimaera and know that no man has ever fought with that monster and lived. For it is a more terrible beast than you would believe. The head and shoulders are those of a lion, the body is that of a goat, and the back parts are those of a dragon. It fights with hot breath and a long tail. She stays on the mountains by night, and goes down into the valleys by day.

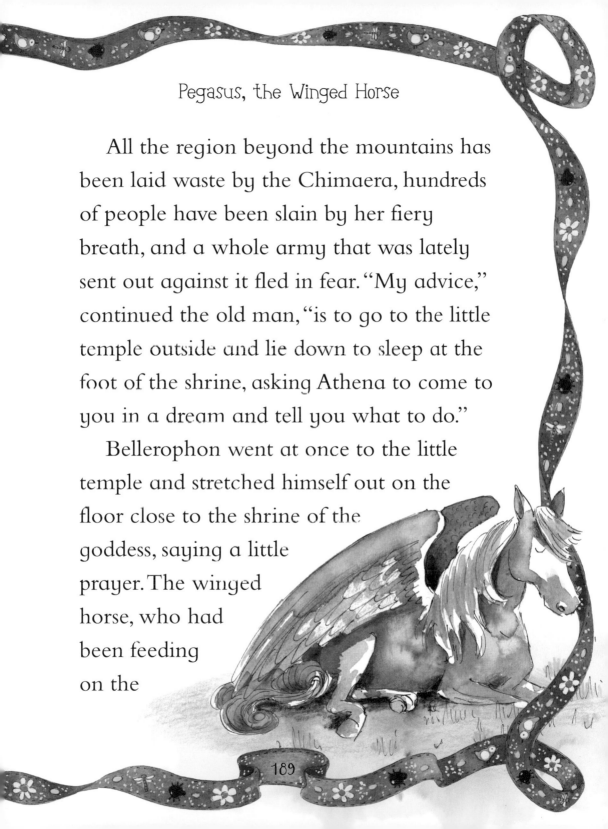

Pegasus, the Winged Horse

All the region beyond the mountains has been laid waste by the Chimaera, hundreds of people have been slain by her fiery breath, and a whole army that was lately sent out against it fled in fear. "My advice," continued the old man, "is to go to the little temple outside and lie down to sleep at the foot of the shrine, asking Athena to come to you in a dream and tell you what to do."

Bellerophon went at once to the little temple and stretched himself out on the floor close to the shrine of the goddess, saying a little prayer. The winged horse, who had been feeding on the grass, followed him and then lay down on the ground outside.

It was nearly morning when Bellerophon dreamed that a tall and stately lady came into the temple and stood beside him.

"Do you know who the winged steed is that waits outside for you?" she asked.

"I do not," answered Bellerophon. "But if I had some means of making him understand me, he might be my best friend and helper."

"His name is Pegasus," said the lady, "and he was born near the shore of the great western ocean. He has come to help you fight with the Chimaera. You can guide him anywhere if you put this ribbon into his mouth and hold on tightly to the ends."

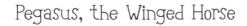

With these words, she placed a beautiful bridle in Bellerophon's hands, and then walked silently away.

When the sun had risen and Bellerophon awoke, the bridle was lying on the floor beside him, and near it was a long bow with arrows and a shield. It was the first bridle that he had ever seen – indeed, some people believe it was the first ever bridle to be made. The young man examined it with great curiosity.

Then he went out and quickly slipped the ribbon bit into the mouth of Pegasus, and leaped upon his back. To his great joy, Bellerophon saw that now the horse understood all of his wishes.

"Here are your bow and arrows and

your shield," cried the old man, handing them to him. "Take them, and may Athena be with you in your fight against the Chimaera!"

At a word from Bellerophon, Pegasus rose high in the air and then, turning, made straight northwards towards the great mountains.

It was evening when they arrived, and quite dark when they at last hovered over the spot that the Chimaera was said to visit at night.

Bellerophon couldn't see the monster until a burning mountain sent out a great sheet of flame, which lit up the valleys. The light gave him a plain view of the Chimaera crouching in the shadow of a cliff. He fitted an arrow quickly in his bow and, as Pegasus paused above the edge of the cliff, flew directly at its fearful head.

The arrow missed the mark and struck the beast in the throat, giving it an ugly wound. Then you should have seen the fury of the Chimaera, how it reared up on its hind feet, how it leaped into the air, how it beat the rocks with its long dragon's tail, how it puffed and fumed and roared and blew its fiery breath towards Pegasus, hoping to scorch his wings or smother both horse and rider with its poisonous fumes.

"Now, my good Pegasus," Bellerophon cried, stroking the horse's mane, "steady yourself just out of her reach and let me send her another gift!"

This time the arrow struck the beast in the back, which only made it more furious than ever. It attacked everything in its reach, clawed the rocks, knocked down trees with its tail, and filled all the mountain-valleys with the noise of mad roaring.

However, Bellerophon's third arrow pierced the horrid creature to the heart. The Chimaera fell backwards lifeless, and rolled over and over down the steep mountainside, and far out into the valley below.

Bellerophon slept on the mountainside that night, while his faithful steed kept watch by his side.

In the morning he went down and found the Chimaera lying stiff and dead in the spot where she had rolled, while a score of

gaping countrymen stood around at a safe distance, rejoicing.

Bellerophon cut off the creature's head, and remounting Pegasus, set out on his journey home.

But at length, an idea struck Bellerophon – why shouldn't he leave this world and ride on the back of Pegasus all the way to the gates of heaven?

And he would have surely have got there if the great god Zeus hadn't noticed him just as he was about to enter. Angered by Bellerophon's boldness, Zeus sent a gadfly to sting the horse. Pegasus made a wild plunge to escape the fly, and Bellerophon, taken by surprise, tumbled back down to the earth.

Very strangely, the hero was not killed by

this long fall, but he was blinded. The majestic Pegasus flew off into the distance, never to be heard of or seen again.

Sigurd the Hero and his Good Horse Grani

By Andrew Lang

Sigurd and his horse, Grani, are heroes of Norse mythology – the ancient stories of the Vikings. Their tale was passed down for generations by storytellers who told it aloud, before it was written down in an Icelandic book called the Volsunga Saga, *over 700 years ago.*

ONCE UPON A TIME there was a king in the north who had won many wars. He was very old, but he took a beautiful young princess to be his new wife.

However, in the midst of his happiness, a

jealous king who had wanted to marry the princess himself came up against him with a great army.

The old king went out and fought bravely, but eventually his sword broke and he was gravely wounded. Sad to say, all his men fled, leaving him for dead.

But in the night, when the battle was over, his young wife came out and searched for him among the slain. At last she found him and asked whether he might be healed. But he said no, his luck was gone, his sword was broken, and he must die. He then told her that she would have a son, and that son would be a great warrior, and he would avenge his death.

He bade her keep the broken pieces of

the sword, to make a new sword for his son, and that blade should be called Gram.

Then he died.

The wife's maid then came up to her and said, "In case the enemy finds us, we must change clothes – you pretend to be me and I will pretend to be you."

So they swapped clothes, and hid together in a nearby wood. It wasn't long, however, before they were discovered and captured by strangers, who carried them away in a ship to Denmark.

There, when they were brought before the king, he thought the maid looked like a queen, and the queen like a maid. So he asked the queen, "How do you know in the dark of night whether morning is near?"

And she said, "I know because, when I was younger, I used to have to rise and light the fires, and still I wake at the same time."

'A strange queen to light the fires,' thought the king.

Then he asked the queen, who was dressed like a maid, "How do you know in the dark of night whether morning is drawing near?"

"My father gave me a gold ring," said she, "and it always grows cold on my finger when dawn comes."

"It would be a very strange house if the maids wore gold!" said the king. "Truly you are no maid, but a king's daughter."

Fortunately he was a good man, who treated her as royalty should be.

NOBLE STEEDS

As time went on the queen had a son,
who she called Sigurd. He was a beautiful
boy and very strong. Sigurd had a tutor to
look after him and teach him about all
things. One day, the tutor told Sigurd to go
to the king and ask for a horse.

"Go and choose one – you can have any
one you like," said the king.

But Sigurd did not go to the royal
stables, as might be expected. Instead, he
went out into the wood where all the wild
horses grazed. There he met an old man
with a white beard, and he said to him,
"Come! Help me choose a horse."

So the old man said, "Drive all the horses
into the river and choose the one that
swims across."

So Sigurd drove them, and only one swam across, and that was the one that Sigurd chose. Unbeknown to Sigurd, the old man was the father of the gods, Odin, and the horse Sigurd had chosen had been bred from Odin's own horse, Sleipnir. Sigurd called him Grani, and he proved to be the best horse on all the earth, as swift as the wind.

NOBLE STEEDS

When Sigurd had grown to be a warrior, he heard a story that somewhere to the south, far away, there was a beautiful lady under a spell. She had to sleep in a castle, surrounded by a flaming fire until a knight could come and rescue her.

Sigurd decided to go there and end the enchantment. He strapped on the sword, Gram, that had been forged from his father's blade, and then sprang onto the good horse Grani. They rode off southwards together into the unknown lands.

After many nights, Sigurd saw a red fire blazing on the crest of a hill, up into the sky. Within the flames, there was a castle with a banner flying from the topmost tower. Sigurd headed towards the fire, and

Sigurd the Hero and his Good Horse Grani

Grani leaped fearlessly through it.

Sigurd went through the castle door and there he saw someone sleeping, all clad in armour. He took the helmet off the head of the sleeper, and there was the beautiful lady. She awoke at once and said, "Ah! Is it Sigurd who has broken the spell at last?"

So thanks to the courage of Sigurd and his good horse Grani, the curse was lifted. The beautiful lady and Sigurd loved each other, and promised to be true to each other forever more.

RIDE LIKE THE WIND

The Enchanted Horse

From *The Arabian Nights* by Andrew Lang

ONE DAY, AN INDIAN MAN presented himself before the King of Persia. He appeared in the throne room leading a life-size model of a horse, richly harnessed, and looking exactly like a real one.

"Sire," said he, bowing to the floor, "I can

promise that no wonder you have ever seen can be compared to this horse. I have only to mount him and wish myself in some special place and, no matter how distant it may be, in a very few moments I shall be there. Let me prove it to you."

The King of Persia was very curious. "Do you see that mountain?" he asked, pointing far off. "Go and bring me the leaf of a palm that grows at its foot."

These words were hardly out of the king's mouth when the man turned a screw in the horse's neck, and the animal bounded away like lightning up into the air and out of sight.

In only a quarter of an hour the man was seen returning, carrying the palm leaf.

Guiding his horse to the foot of the throne, he dismounted, and graciously laid the leaf before the king.

"I must own this miraculous horse!" cried the king. "Name your price – you can have anything you like! Gold, jewels, a palace, a city – anything!"

The king and the man were so busy haggling over the price that neither of them noticed the king's son swing himself up onto the horse's back. Prince Firouz (for that was his name) wanted to see the horse's amazing powers for himself. Quietly, he found the screw, turned it, soared into the air, and was soon out of sight.

The stunned king and the Indian man waited for the prince to return. They waited… and waited… and waited… but there was no sign of him.

"Sire," the man explained anxiously, "Your son took off before I could tell him about the second screw, which makes the horse come back."

"Well, I hold you responsible for whatever happens!" cried the king, and ordered his guards to seize the man and throw him into prison.

Meanwhile, Prince Firouz had gone excitedly up into the air, higher and higher, before deciding it was time to come down. He thought that he would simply have to turn the screw the other way. But to his surprise and horror he found it had no effect at all! Luckily he stayed calm and at

last discovered a second peg, close to the horse's right ear.

This he turned and found himself dropping slowly down to the earth.

It was now dark and the prince had no idea where he was. By the light of the moon, he could just see that he seemed to be on the flat roof of a huge palace. He opened a small door

and found himself going down a staircase into the palace itself.

He crept through a faintly lit hall in which many guards, armed with swords, were sleeping. Beyond, he found himself in a magnificent chamber full of sleeping women, all lying on low mattresses except for one who was on a splendid bed, and this one, he knew, must be a princess.

The prince tiptoed near to see her. She was more beautiful than any woman he had ever seen!

At that very moment, the princess opened her eyes. Luckily for the prince, she was too astonished to scream. He fell to his knees and told the princess who he was. He assured her that he meant her no harm and told her the amazing tale of how he came to be there.

The princess, who was the daughter of the King of Bengal, listened in wonder. Being clever as well as beautiful, she could tell that he was speaking the truth, but she thought it best to wait till the morning to decide what to do. She woke her maids and ordered them to take the prince to a guest room, where he could eat and rest.

Next morning, the princess made sure she looked her absolute best and went to see Prince Firouz.

"Thank you for the kindness you have shown me," the prince said. "I have nothing but my heart to offer you — although it was yours from the first moment I beheld you. I want nothing more than to present myself at the court of your father, the king, and ask for your hand in marriage. But alas, I am unable to do so as a wanderer. I can only do this properly, bringing gifts and servants as the Prince of Persia… Besides, I cannot stay – my father must be extremely worried."

The Princess of Bengal was dreadfully upset. She said that the only way she would let Prince Firouz go was if she went with him. So, that night, when the whole palace was wrapped in sleep, the prince and princess flew off on the enchanted horse, back to Persia.

The prince landed at a country house a short journey away from the palace. While the princess rested and prepared herself to meet the king, the prince rode off to the palace to announce their arrival.

The king was overjoyed to see his son back safely. The prince told all that had happened and his father embraced him, eagerly, saying "My son, not only do I gladly consent to your marriage with the Princess of Bengal, but I will hurry to meet her, so the wedding can be celebrated straight away."

The prince was overjoyed and went off to order preparations for the wedding.

But before the king set off for the country house to fetch the princess, he ordered the Indian man to be brought from prison before him. "Fortunately for you,"

said the king, "my son has now returned –
so take your horse, and be gone for ever!"

The relieved man hastily scurried away
before the king could change his mind. But
as soon as he was outside the throne room
he asked the servants where the prince had
been and what he had been doing. They
told him the whole story.

Then the man had the idea for a nasty
plan. He went straight to the country house
and informed the doorkeeper who was left
in charge that he had been sent by the king
and prince to fetch the princess on the
enchanted horse, and to bring her to the
palace. Soon, he was soaring into the skies
on the back of the enchanted horse, stealing
away the Princess of Bengal!

RIDE LIKE THE WIND

When the king and his son discovered what had happened, they were appalled. Prince Firouz set out at once to find his beloved princess, even though he had no idea in which direction he should search.

Meanwhile the horse flew all the way to the kingdom of Cashmere. The man brought it down in a wood near the capital city, so the princess could drink from a shady stream while he went to find food.

You can imagine the princess's horror at what had happened! She started shouting and calling for help, and luckily her cries were heard by a troop of horsemen led by the Sultan of Cashmere.

The Enchanted Horse

The sultan promised to help the princess
and took her, and the enchanted horse
back to his palace.

However, little did the princess
know that the sultan had no
intention of returning her to her
beloved prince. No, he had
made up his mind to have her
as his own wife! The very next
day, the sultan ordered their
wedding to be announced
throughout the city.

The Princess of Bengal was
awakened by the noise and was so
horrified when she realized what
was happening that she sank down
in a dead faint. As she gradually

came to, she came up with a clever plan.
She realized that if she pretended to be
mad, the sultan would not marry her. So
from that moment on, that is what she did.

Days passed, and the princess seemed to
have totally lost her wits. The Sultan of
Cashmere summoned every doctor from far
and wide to see her – but none seemed to
be able to help.

During this time, Prince Firouz arrived in
a city where he heard talk about the
Princess of Bengal who had gone out of her
senses. At once, he hurried as fast as he
could to the capital city. The very next day,
he dressed as a doctor and presented himself
at the palace, promising that he could cure
the princess where all others had failed. The

prince was shown into the princess's presence and his heart leaped for joy. He knew at once that she was pretending. And she knew at once that the new doctor was in fact her beloved prince. But neither of them gave anything away, for fear of being flung into prison – or worse.

Instead, the prince asked the sultan to tell the story of how the princess came to be in such a sorry state. The sultan explained everything and the prince nodded his head wisely. "Ah, that's just as I suspected," he said mysteriously. "During the princess's trip on the enchanted horse, part of its enchantment has passed into her. I need to put the magic that is making her mad, back into the horse. If Your Highness can bring both the princess and the horse into the big square outside the palace, I promise that in a very few moments, you shall see the princess as healthy both in mind and body as she was before."

The sultan excitedly agreed to all that the prince proposed and soon everyone was standing in the big square outside the palace, surrounded by a big, curious crowd. The Princess of Bengal was helped onto the enchanted horse by her maids. Then, muttering magic words, the 'doctor' placed metal pots of burning coals around them. Everyone gasped as he threw on powders, which blew up great clouds of thick smoke. This was the moment he had been waiting for. The prince jumped up behind the

princess, leaned
forwards and turned the peg,
and the horse sprang up into the air and
soared away.

It was in this way that the Prince of
Persia rescued the Princess of Bengal, and
returned with her to Persia, where they
landed in the grounds of the palace. The

marriage was held as soon as the princess's father, the Sultan of Bengal, was able to reach Persia, and they all lived happily ever after – though they never again flew on the enchanted horse.

The Dun Horse

Edited by Hamilton Wright Mabie

*This story is a Native American folktale. The Pawnee were
a farming people who lived around the Missouri River, in modern-
day Nebraska and northern Kansas in the United States.*

MANY YEARS AGO, there lived in the
Pawnee tribe an old woman and her
sixteen-year-old grandson. They had no
relations and were very poor – so poor that
they were looked down on by the rest of the
tribe. They had nothing of their own, so
always, after the village started to move the

camp from one place to another, these two
would stay behind, to pick up anything that
the other Indians had thrown away.

Now, it happened one day, after the tribe
had moved away from the camp, that
this old woman and her boy were following
along the trail behind the rest, when they
came to a miserable old dun horse.

The poor old thing was exhausted. He
was blind in one eye, and had a bad back.
In fact, he was so downtrodden that none of
the Pawnees had been willing to take the
trouble to try to drive him along with them.
He had been left behind.

But when the old woman and her boy
came along, the boy said, "Come now, we
will take this poor old horse, and care for

him – he can help us carry our pack."

So the old woman put her pack on the horse and drove him along, though he limped and could only go very slowly.

The tribe moved on until they came to Court House Rock. The two poor Indians followed them and camped with the others. One day soon after, the news spread that a large herd of buffalo were near and that among them was a spotted calf.

The Head Chief of the Pawnees had a very beautiful daughter, and when he heard about the spotted calf, he ordered his old crier to go about through the village and call out that the man who killed the spotted calf should have his daughter for his wife. To have a spotted robe was a very grand thing indeed within the Pawnee tribe.

So all the warriors and the young men picked out their best and fastest horses, and made ready to charge upon the herd.

Among them was the poor boy on the old dun horse. But when they saw him, all the rich young braves on their fast horses pointed at him and laughed, so that the

poor boy was ashamed, and rode off to one side of the crowd, where he could not hear their cruel joking and teasing.

When they stopped, the horse turned his head round and said to the boy in a quiet voice, "Do not ride back to the warriors who laugh at you because you have such a poor horse. Stay right here until the word is given to charge." The boy was so surprised to hear a talking horse that he did as he was told and stayed there.

Presently all the fine horses were drawn up in line and pranced about, and they were so eager to go that their riders could hardly hold them in. At last the old crier gave the word, "Loo-ah!" – Go!

The Pawnees all leaned forwards on their

horses and yelled, and away they went as fast as the could possibly go.

The old dun horse did not seem to run. Instead he seemed to sail along like a graceful bird. He passed all the fastest horses and in a moment was among the buffalo. The boy easily picked out the spotted calf and, charging up alongside of it, let loose an arrow, straight and true. The calf fell instantly. Then the boy drew another arrow, which took down a large cow.

The boy slid off the back of the old dun horse to the ground – but how changed the animal was! He pranced about and would hardly stand still. His back was all right again, his legs were well and fine, and both his eyes were clear and bright.

RIDE LIKE THE WIND

The boy skinned the calf and the cow, and made two robes, then he prepared all the meat carefully and packed it up for the horse to carry. The boy put the spotted robe on the very top of the load, and started back to the camp on foot leading the dun horse. Even with this heavy load the horse pranced all the time!

On the way back to the camp, one of the rich young chiefs of the tribe rode up by the boy and offered him twelve good horses for the spotted robe, so that he could marry the Head Chief's beautiful daughter, but the boy laughed at him and would not sell.

Now the other warriors got back to camp shortly before the boy. They went to the old woman and said to her, "Your grandson has killed the spotted calf."

And the old woman said, "Why do you come to tell me this? You ought to be ashamed. Why make fun of my boy, just because he is poor?"

Then the old woman began to cry. But soon the boy came along leading the young-looking, prancing dun horse, and she was very surprised. The boy said to her, "Here, I have brought you plenty of meat to eat, and here is a robe, that you may have for yourself." Then the old woman laughed, for her heart was glad.

That night the horse spoke again to the boy and said, "Now lead me off, far away behind that big hill, and leave me there tonight, and in the morning come for me."

The boy did as he was told and when he went for the horse in the morning, he found with him a beautiful white gelding, much more handsome than any horse in the tribe.

That night the dun horse told the boy to take him again to the place behind the big hill and to come for him the next morning, and when the boy went for him again, he found with him a beautiful black gelding.

And so for ten nights, he left the horse among the hills, and each morning he found a different coloured horse – a bay, a roan, a grey, a blue, a spotted horse, and all of them finer than any horses that the Pawnees had ever had in their tribe before.

When the boy grew up he married the beautiful daughter of the Head Chief, and

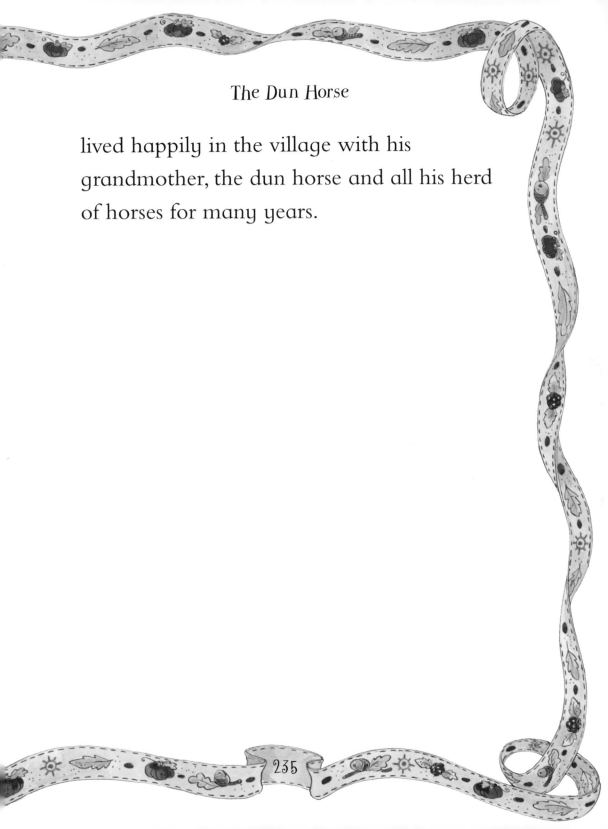

The Dun Horse

lived happily in the village with his grandmother, the dun horse and all his herd of horses for many years.

The Magician's Horse

By Andrew Lang

ONCE UPON A TIME there was a king who had three sons. One day the three princes went hunting in a large forest that was quite far from the palace. After a time the youngest prince became separated from his brothers and he lost his way. The two other princes were very worried, but when night fell they had no choice but to return home without him.

For four long days the youngest prince wandered through the forest, sleeping on moss and living on roots and wild berries. He knew he must be far away from the palace and was becoming very worried. At last, on the morning of the fifth day, he came to a large open space in the middle of the forest, and here stood a stately palace.

The prince entered the open door and wandered through the many rooms – they were completely deserted and there was no sign of life.

At last he came to a great hall where a table was spread with dainty dishes and fine wines. The prince sat down and satisfied his hunger and thirst, but as soon as he put down his knife and fork the table disappeared from his sight!

This struck the prince as very, very strange — he couldn't believe his eyes. But even though he continued his search through all the rooms, upstairs and down, he could find no one to speak to.

At last, just as it was beginning to get dark outside, he heard steps echoing from somewhere in the palace, and then he saw an old man coming towards him up the grand stairs.

"What are you doing wandering about my castle?" asked the old man.

The prince quickly replied, "I lost my way, hunting in the forest. If you will take

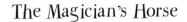

me into your service, I will stay with you and serve you faithfully."

"Very well," said the old man. "You will have to keep the stove alight all day and night. You can fetch the wood for it from the forest, and you must look after the black horse in the stables. I will pay you a gold coin a day, and at meal times you will always find the table in thc hall spread with food and wine for you."

The prince knew he was completely lost, and couldn't find his way home, so he was satisfied to enter the old man's service.

Though he did not know it, his master was actually a magician, and the flame of the stove was a magic fire – if it went out he would lose a great part of his power.

RIDE LIKE THE WIND

One day while the magician was out the prince was working in the stables, grooming the magician's horse, when to his great surprise it spoke to him!

"Come into my stall," it said. "Fetch my bridle and saddle and put them on me. Then take the bottle that is beside them – it contains an ointment that will make your hair shine like pure gold. Then pile all the wood you can gather together onto the stove."

The Magician's Horse

The prince was very surprised to hear a talking horse, but he did what it told him. He put the bridle and saddle on the horse, used the oil to make his hair shine, and in a few minutes, there was such a big fire in the stove that the flames sprang up and set fire to the roof. The palace was burning like a bonfire.

Then the prince hurried back to the stables and the horse said to him, "Fetch me a looking-glass, a brush and a riding-whip, climb on my back, and ride as hard as you can away from here."

The prince did as the horse bade him, and in a short time, the forest and all the country belonging to the magician lay far behind them.

RIDE LIKE THE WIND

In the meantime the magician returned to his palace, which he found in burning ruins, with his servant and his horse gone. Enraged, he instantly mounted a roan horse from his stables and set out in pursuit.

As the prince rode, the quick ears of the horse heard the sound of the magician coming after them. "Throw the looking-glass on the ground," said the horse. So the prince threw it and when the magician caught up, his roan horse stepped on the mirror. Crash! His foot went through the glass. There was nothing for the old man to do but go back with the horse to the stables and put new shoes on its feet.

When the prince had gone a great distance, the quick ears of the horse heard the sound of following feet once more. "Throw the brush on the ground," it said.

And so the prince threw it, and in an instant the brush was changed into such a thick wood that even a bird could not have got through it.

When the old magician came riding up to the wood he came suddenly to a standstill – he wasn't able to advance a step into the thick tangle. There was nothing for the magician to do but to retrace his steps to fetch an axe, with which he returned and chopped a way through the wood.

Then once more the quick ears of the horse heard the sound of pursuing feet. "Throw down the whip," instructed the horse. And in the twinkling of an eye the whip was changed into a broad river.

When the old man reached the water he urged the roan horse into the river, but as the water mounted higher, the magic flame back at the palace that gave the magician all his power burned smaller and smaller, until, with a fizz, it went out, and the old man and the roan horse disappeared. When the prince looked round they could no longer be seen.

"Now," said the horse, "you may dismount. There is nothing more to fear, for the magician has gone. Beside that brook you will find a willow wand. Pick it up then strike the earth with it. The ground will open up, and you will see a door at your feet, which leads to a large stone hall. Take

me into it – I will stay there but you must
go to the gardens beyond, in the midst of
which is a king's palace. When you get
there you must ask to be taken into the
king's service."

The horse also made the prince promise
not to let anyone in the palace see his
golden hair. So the prince bound a long
scarf around it, like a turban, and did
everything the horse had instructed him to
do. He left the horse in the stone hall, then
went into the palace garden and asked the
royal gardener for a job.

From then on, the prince worked all day,
weeding and hoeing, and he enjoyed his
new work. But whenever his food was given
to him he only ate half of it – the rest he

carried to the hall beside the brook, and
gave it to the horse, who thanked him for
his faithful friendship.

One evening, when they were sitting
together in the stone hall, the horse said to
him, "Tomorrow a large company of
princes and great lords are coming to your
king's palace, to woo his three daughters.
They will all stand in a row in the
courtyard of the palace, and the three
princesses will come out.

Each will carry a diamond apple in her
hand, which she will throw into the air. The
man whose feet the apple falls at will be the
bridegroom of that princess. You must be
close by, working in the garden. The apple
of the youngest princess, who is the most

beautiful, will roll past the wooers and stop in front of you. Pick it up at once and put it in your pocket."

The next day, everything happened just as the horse had said – the youngest princess threw her apple and it landed at the prince's feet – but just as he stooped to pick it up, the scarf round his head slipped a

little to one side, and the princess caught sight of his golden hair. From that very moment she loved him.

The next day, a threefold wedding was celebrated at the palace – all three sisters were married.

After the wedding, the youngest princess returned with her new husband, the prince, to the small hut in the garden where he lived, and they were very happy together there for some time.

After a few months, the king went away to war with a distant country. He was accompanied by the husbands of his two eldest daughters and his army.

The king thought that the youngest daughter's husband was only a gardener

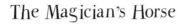

without a horse — he wouldn't be of any use on the battlefield and must stay behind.

But when the prince heard that he had been left behind he hurried to the horse in the stone hall.

The horse said to him, "Go into the next room and you will find a suit of armour and a sword. Put them on, and we will ride forth together and join the king in battle."

The prince did as he was told, and when he had mounted the horse he looked so brave and handsome, that no one would have ever recognized him as the palace gardener.

Then the horse bore the prince away swiftly to the battlefield. He fought so bravely and boldly with his sword that none could stand against him.

When the enemy saw the terrifying
warrior in his glittering armour on his

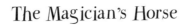

horse, they scattered and fled.

Then the king and his two sons-in-law rejoiced and ran to thank the strange knight. The king saw that the knight's leg was wounded and hurried to bind it with his own pocket handkerchief, which had the royal crown embroidered up on it.

They would have escorted him straight back to the palace – but, to their astonishment, the horse rose up and bore the stranger out of their sight. Then they all shouted and cried, "The warrior who has fought for us must be a god!"

Throughout all the kingdom nothing else was spoken about, and all the people said, "Who can the hero be who has fought for all of us?"

And the king said, "If only I could see him once more, I would reward him with half my kingdom."

Now when the prince reached the gardener's hut where he lived with his wife he was weary, and he lay down on his bed and slept. His wife noticed the handkerchief bound round his wounded leg, and she wondered what it could be. She looked at it more closely and saw in the corner that it was embroidered with the royal crown.

She ran straight to the palace and told her father. The king and his two sons-in-law followed her back to her house, and there the gardener lay asleep on his bed. And the scarf that he always wore bound round his head had slipped off and his golden hair gleamed on the pillow. And they all recognized that this was the hero who had won the battle for them.

Then there was great celebrating throughout the land and the king rewarded his son-in-law with half of his kingdom, and he and his wife reigned happily over it for the rest of their days, with the wise horse as their companion.

Al Borak

By James Baldwin

The religion of Islam tells stories about a wonderful flying horse, which the angel Gabriel (or Jibril) delivered from heaven. Here, the horse carries the prophet Muhammad on a famous quest often known as the Night Journey.

A L BORAK is an Arabic name, which means 'the Lightning'. This is the story of a wondrous steed with that name.

It was midnight, thirteen hundred years ago, and Muhammad, the prophet, lay asleep in his house in the ancient city of Mecca. Suddenly he was roused by a loud voice crying, "Up, up, sleeper! Arise and make ready for your journey!"

Muhammad leaped to his feet and looked around. Before him stood a dazzling creature he took to be an angel. His face was white as the purest marble, his hair was of gold and fell in silk-like waves about his shoulders, his wings reflected all the colours of the rainbow, and his robes of spotless white were embroidered with gold and thickly set with precious gems.

Muhammad was about to speak when he saw that the angel was holding the reins of the most marvellous steed that any man had ever beheld.

It appeared to be a horse and yet it was not like a horse. Its limbs were slender and

long, its body was strong and finely formed,
its coat sleek and glossy, and its mane so
long that it almost swept the ground. Its
colour was white, intermingled with
golden-yellow, and there was a golden star
in its forehead. Folded over its back were
wings like those of an eagle, amid the

plumes of which lightning gleamed and flashed. Its eyes were brighter than burning coals of fire, its ears were sharp-pointed and restless, its nostrils were wide and steaming — and it spoke with a human voice in the purest Arabic.

Muhammad had no sooner seen this wonderful steed than he was filled with a desire to ride it. But when he reached forth his hand and made ready to spring upon its back, it reared high in the air, and would have struck at the prophet with its golden hoofs had not the angel restrained it.

"Be still, Al Borak!" cried the angel. "Do you not know who you oppose? It is Muhammad, the son of Abdallah, of one of the tribes of Arabia the Happy. He is the prophet of Allah and through his prayers any creature can enter paradise."

Al Borak at once became as gentle as a lamb and allowed the prophet to mount upon her back. Rising gently from the ground, she soared aloft above the desert sands and mountains of Arabia. The night was dark – the darkest that any man ever knew, and it was so still that all nature seemed as though it was sleeping.

There was no sound anywhere of stirring wind or of rippling water. No chirp of wakeful insect, no rustle of creeping reptile, no baying of dogs, no howling of wild beasts among the mountains disturbed the solemn hour. All Arabia was quiet – as silent as the grave. And Al Borak, with face directed northwards, and at a speed that outdistanced thought, sailed noiselessly through the gloom.

Only three times did the steed alight upon the earth – first upon Mount Sinai, then in the village of Bethlehem, and finally at the gate of the temple in Jerusalem. There Muhammad dismounted, and, fastening the steed to a ring that was attached to one of the stones of the temple, he left her and went in to pray.

When, at length, he returned to the gate of the temple, he found the steed in the place where he had tethered her, and, having remounted her, was carried in an instant back to Mecca and set down at his own door.

RIDE LIKE THE WIND

Then Al Borak, having bowed low in honor of the prophet, unfolded her wings again and soared aloft into the upper air. She flew away, never again to be seen by mortal man.

The distance from Mecca to Jerusalem is about eight hundred miles as the crow flies, or as Al Borak flew. And yet, although Muhammad had not stopped at Jerusalem, but had gone some millions of miles beyond, the whole affair was accomplished in less time than you can think of it.

It is easy to prove that this was so. In the first hurry of setting out, a vase of water had been overturned by the angel's wing, but Muhammad returned in time to catch the falling vessel before its contents could be spilled. Could anything have been quicker? Not even thought or a flash of light could have outsped Al Borak.

Going
for the
Doctor

From *Black Beauty* by Anna Sewell

In this extract from Black Beauty *the young horse lives on the country estate of a wealthy landowner called Squire Gordon, whose wife is dangerously ill. Here, Black Beauty saves the day despite being placed in grave danger.*

O NE NIGHT, I had eaten my hay and was lying down in my straw fast asleep, when I was suddenly roused by the stable bell ringing very loudly. I heard the door of the coachman's house open and the feet of my groom, John, running up the drive to the squire's hall.

He was back again in no time – he unlocked the stable door and came in, calling out, "Wake up, Beauty! You must go fast now, if ever you did."

Almost before I could think, he had got the saddle on my back and the bridle on my head, and he then took me at a quick trot up to the hall door.

Squire Gordon stood there, with a lamp in his hand. "Now, John," he said, "ride for your life – that is, for your mistress's life, there is not a moment to lose. Give this note to Dr White, then give your horse a rest at the inn and be back as soon as you can."

John said, "Yes, sir," and was on my back in a minute.

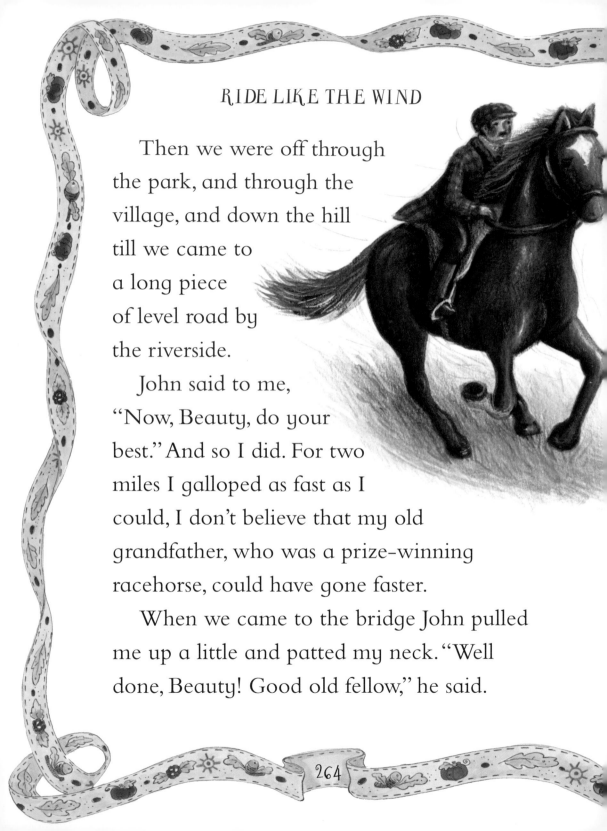

RIDE LIKE THE WIND

Then we were off through the park, and through the village, and down the hill till we came to a long piece of level road by the riverside.

John said to me, "Now, Beauty, do your best." And so I did. For two miles I galloped as fast as I could, I don't believe that my old grandfather, who was a prize-winning racehorse, could have gone faster.

When we came to the bridge John pulled me up a little and patted my neck. "Well done, Beauty! Good old fellow," he said.

He would have let me go slower, but my spirit was up, and I was off again, galloping as fast as before.

After eight miles' run we came to the town, through the streets and into the market place. It was all quite still except the clatter of my feet on the stones – everybody was asleep. The church clock struck three as we drew up at Dr White's door. John rang the bell twice and then knocked at the door like thunder. A window was thrown up and Dr White, in his nightcap, put his head out and said, "What do you want?"

"Mrs Gordon is very ill, sir. Master wants you to come at once – he thinks she will die if you cannot get there. Here is a note."

"Wait," he said, "I will come."

He shut the window and was soon at the door to speak to John.

"The worst of it is," he said, "that my horse has been out all day and is quite exhausted, my son has my other one and he is away. What is to be done? Can I have your horse?"

"He has come at a gallop nearly all the way, sir, and I was to give him a rest here – but I think my master would not be against it, if you think fit, sir."

"All right," the doctor said, "I will soon be ready to go."

John stood by me and stroked my neck. I was very hot. The doctor came out with his riding-whip.

"You need not take that, sir," said John,

"Black Beauty will go till he drops. Take care of him, sir, if you can. I should not like any harm to come to him."

"Of course, John," said the doctor, and in a minute we had left John far behind.

I will not tell about our way back. The doctor was a heavier man than John and not so good a rider, however, I did my very best. By the time we reached the park, I was very nearly spent. The groom's boy, Joe, was at the lodge gate and my master was at the hall door, waiting. My master spoke not a word as the doctor went into the house with him. Then Joe led me to the stable.

I was glad to get home – my legs shook under me and I could only stand and pant. I had not a dry hair on my body, the sweat

ran down my legs and I steamed all over.
Joe was young and small, but he did the
very best for me that he knew. He rubbed
my legs and chest, but he did not put my
warm cloth on me – he thought I was so
hot I should not like it.

Then he gave me a pailful of water to
drink. It was cold and very good, and I
drank it all. Then he gave me some hay and
some corn and, thinking he had done right,
he went away.

Soon I began to shake and tremble and
turned deadly cold. My legs ached, my loins
ached, and my chest ached, and I felt sore
all over. Oh, how I wished for my warm
thick cloth, as I stood and trembled! I
wished for John, but he had eight miles to

walk, so I lay down in my straw and tried to go to sleep.

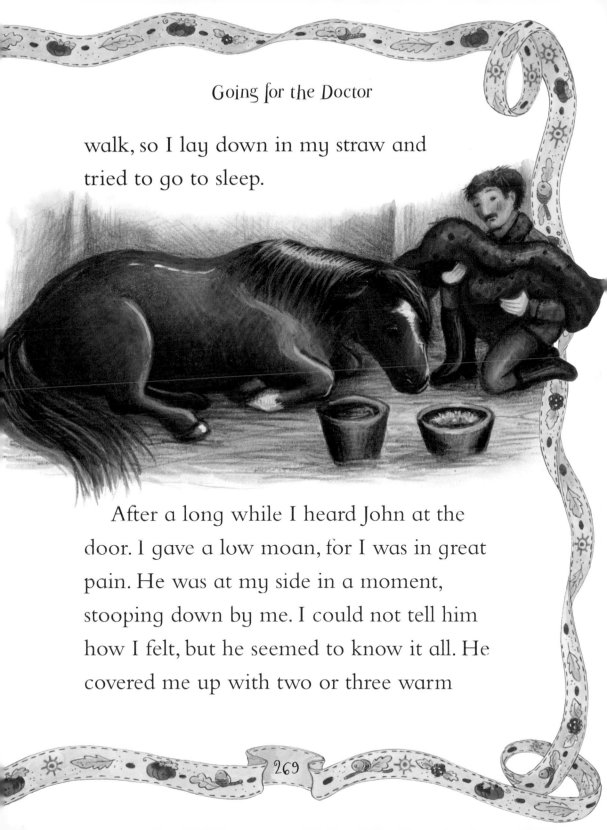

After a long while I heard John at the door. I gave a low moan, for I was in great pain. He was at my side in a moment, stooping down by me. I could not tell him how I felt, but he seemed to know it all. He covered me up with two or three warm cloths and then ran to the house for some hot water. He made me some warm gruel, which I drank, and then I fell fast asleep.

The next day, I became very ill. A strong inflammation attacked my lungs, and I could not draw my breath without pain. John nursed me round the clock – he would get up two or three times in the night to come to me. My master, too, often came to see me, until I was better.

"My poor Beauty," he said one day, "my good horse, you saved your mistress's life, Beauty. Yes, you saved her life." I was very glad to hear that.

Apparently, the doctor had said that if we had been a little longer it would have been too late. John told my master he never saw a horse go so fast in his life – that it seemed almost as if I had known what was the matter.

Of course, I had done!

The Prince of Horses

From *Dorothy and the Wizard in Oz*
by L Frank Baum

This story comes from the fourth book L Frank Baum wrote about the magical land of Oz. When Dorothy, her cousin Zeb, and her cat Eureka are riding in a buggy being pulled by a cab-horse named Jim, an earthquake opens a crevice in the ground. They fall into a strange fairy country and, after many adventures, they reach Oz.

IN THE AFTERNOON they all went to a great field outside the city gates where the games were to be held. There was a beautiful canopy for Princess Ozma of Oz and her guests to sit under and watch the people run races and jump and wrestle.

The Prince of Horses

The scarecrow proposed a race between the saw-horse and Jim the cab-horse, and although all the others were delighted at the suggestion the saw-horse drew back, saying, "Such a race would not be fair."

"Of course not," added Jim, with a touch of scorn, "those little wooden legs of yours are not half as long as my own."

"It isn't that," said the saw-horse, modestly. "I never tire and you do."

"Bah!" cried Jim, looking with great disdain at the other. "Do you imagine for an instant that such a shabby imitation of a horse as you are can run as fast as I?"

"I don't know, I'm sure," replied the saw-horse with certainty.

"That is what we are trying to find out,"

remarked the scarecrow. "The object of a race is to see who can win it – or at least that is what my excellent brains think."

"Once, when I was young," said Jim, "I was a racehorse and defeated all who dared run against me. I was born in Kentucky, you know, where all the best and most aristocratic horses come from."

"But you're old, now, Jim," suggested Dorothy's friend, Zeb.

"Old! Why, I feel like a colt today," replied Jim. "I only wish there was a real horse here for me to race with. I'd show the people a fine sight, I can tell you."

"Then why not race with the saw-horse?" inquired the scarecrow.

"He's too afraid," said Jim.

"Oh, no," answered the saw-horse. "I merely said it wasn't fair. But if my friend the Real Horse is willing to undertake the race, I am quite ready."

So they unharnessed Jim and took the saddle off the saw-horse, and the two queerly matched animals were stood side by side for the start.

Then Zeb, called out, "When I say 'Go!' you must race off until you reach those three trees you see over yonder. Then circle round them and come back again. The first one that passes the place where the princess sits shall be crowned the winner. Now, are you ready?"

"I suppose I ought to give the wooden dummy a good headstart," growled Jim.

RIDE LIKE THE WIND

"Never mind that," said the saw-horse. "I'll do the best I can."

"Go!" cried Zeb, and at the word the two horses leaped forwards and the race was begun in earnest.

Jim's big hoofs pounded away at a great rate and, although he did not look very graceful, he ran in a way to do credit to his Kentucky breeding.

But the saw-horse was swifter than the wind. Its wooden legs moved so fast that their twinkling could scarcely be seen and, although it was so much smaller than the cab-horse it covered the ground much, much faster.

Before they had reached the trees the saw-horse was far ahead. The wooden

277

animal returned to the starting place and was being lustily cheered by the Ozites before Jim came panting up to the canopy where the princess and her friends were seated together.

Then Princess Ozma took the coronet from her own head and placed it upon that of the winner of the race.

Princess Ozma proclaimed to the saw-horse, "My friend, I reward you for your swiftness by proclaiming you Prince of Horses, whether of wood or of flesh, and hereafter all other horses – in the Land of Oz, at least – must be considered imitations, and you the real champion of your race."

More applause followed, then Princess Ozma had the jewelled saddle placed upon the saw-horse. She herself rode the victor back to the city at the head of the grand procession.

Helios's Four-in-hand

A myth from Ancient Greece
by James Baldwin

JUST HOW LONG THE GOD HELIOS had
been driving the chariot of the sun
nobody could tell – even the oldest man
alive had no recollection of the time when
he began. Helios never missed a day. Every
morning, starting from the home of the
dawn in the far east, he made a daily trip to
the distant west. How it was that he always

got back to his starting-point before the next morning was a mystery. Nobody had ever seen him making his return trip.

Each night, the old charioteer always slept soundly until his young sister, Aurora, rapped at the door of his bedroom and shouted, "Get up Helios! It is time!"

Then Helios would hasten to the meadows where his steeds were feeding and call them, "Come, beautiful creatures! Eös, glowing one! Æthon, with the burning mane! Brontë, thunderer! Sterope, swifter than lightning! All come quickly!"

The wing-footed steeds would obey and servants would harness them tightly to the golden chariot.

Then Helios would step into the chariot

and hold the long, yellow reins in his hands. A word from him and the proud team would leap into the sky. Then they would soar above the mountain tops and mingle with the clouds, with Helios holding the reins steadily.

The wife of Helios was a human named Clymene, who lived not far from the great sea, and they had an only son named Phaëthon. Helios loved this son above all things. Phaëthon grew up tall and handsome – and very proud of who his father was. But some of his companions didn't believe him and were very jealous.

"How dare you call yourself the son of Helios!" scoffed one lad one day.

"But I am!" protested the boy.

RIDE LIKE THE WIND

"Don't talk to us about your father the chariot-driver!" sneered another. "Why, you would be frightened to death to drive your sister's goat-cart over the lawn and you would shriek at the sight of a real horse."

The boys laughed and a group of girls that were passing giggled.

"I'll show you one day!" Phaëthon cried.

"Until you have driven the sun-chariot through the skies, nobody will believe that you are the son of Helios!" one of the ruffians challenged, and they all went on their way laughing.

"You may mock me," said Phaëthon, "but soon you will all be sorry."

From then on, Phaëthon began exercising every day to grow stronger. He

practised running and leaping and throwing
weights, until his muscles were hardened.

Then he took lessons in horsemanship
from the greatest riding-masters. He spent
months on the steppes of the Caspian,
where he learned to lasso wild horses and
ride them barebacked and bridleless. He

entered the chariot races at Corinth and
with a team of four outdrove the most
famous charioteers of Greece.

And at the great Olympic games he won
the victor's crown. No other young man
was talked about as much as he.

At length, Phaëthon made the long
journey to the Palace of the Dawn in the
far distant East. He arrived one night when
Helios had just returned from his labours.
He was overjoyed to see his son. He threw
his arms about him, kissed him many times
and called him by many fond names.

"And now tell me," Helios said, "what
brings you here at this quiet hour of the
night, when all men are asleep. Have you
come to seek some favour? If so, do not be

afraid to tell me – for you know that I will do anything for you – that I will give you anything that you ask."

"There is something," said Phaëthon, "that I long for more than anything else in the world, and I have come to ask you to give it to me."

"What is it, my child?" asked Helios, eagerly. "Only speak and I vow by the most solemn oath of the gods that it shall be yours at once."

Then the delighted young man said, "This, then, O father, is the question that I have come to ask and which you have promised to give – I wish to take your place tomorrow, and drive your chariot through the flaming pathway of the sky."

RIDE LIKE THE WIND

Helios sank back terrified at the request and for a time could not speak.

"My child," he said at last, "you surely do not mean it. No man living can ever drive my steeds, even if he is the son of a god. Choose, I pray you, some other favour."

All through the night Helios pleaded with the young man, but in vain – Phaëthon would not listen. "This is the only favour I will have," said he. "I will drive the sun-chariot through the heavens tomorrow and then all men shall know that I am the son of Helios."

At length Aurora came knocking at the door, and Helios knew that he had run out of time to change his son's mind. He hung his head in despair. The four horses were led out and harnessed to the chariot and Helios sadly placed the reins into his son's hands.

"Your foolishness will bring its own punishment, my son," he said, and, hiding his face in his long cloak, wept.

But the young man leaped eagerly into the chariot and up sprang the four steeds into the blue sky. Madly, they careered above the mountain tops, turning this way and that, taking no notice of their driver, for they could tell that it was not their master who stood in the chariot behind them.

The proud heart of Phaëthon began to tremble. He quaked with fear and the yellow reins dropped from his hands.

"O my father," he cried, "how I wish that I had heeded your warning!"

RIDE LIKE THE WIND

The fiery steeds leaped upwards and soared in the heavens until they reached a point higher than any eagle. Then, as suddenly, they plunged downwards, dragging the burning car behind them. For a long time, they skimmed close to the tree-tops, then dangerously near to villages and towns, and down even lower, scorching huge areas of the earth into barren desert, drying up the rivers.

Then all living creatures, great and small, cried out in their terror, praying to the god Zeus to do something to stop the mad horses before the whole world was destroyed by fire.

From his palace Zeus heard their prayers. He hurled his thunderbolts at

Helios's Four-in-hand

Phaëthon and the youth fell out of the chariot, tumbling down through the skies. The four horses soared up into their rightful place and galloped off on their usual journey. Helios was in the west, awaiting their coming, and when he saw that Phaëthon was not in the chariot deep sorrow filled his heart and he wept.

Phaëthon was never seen again but the

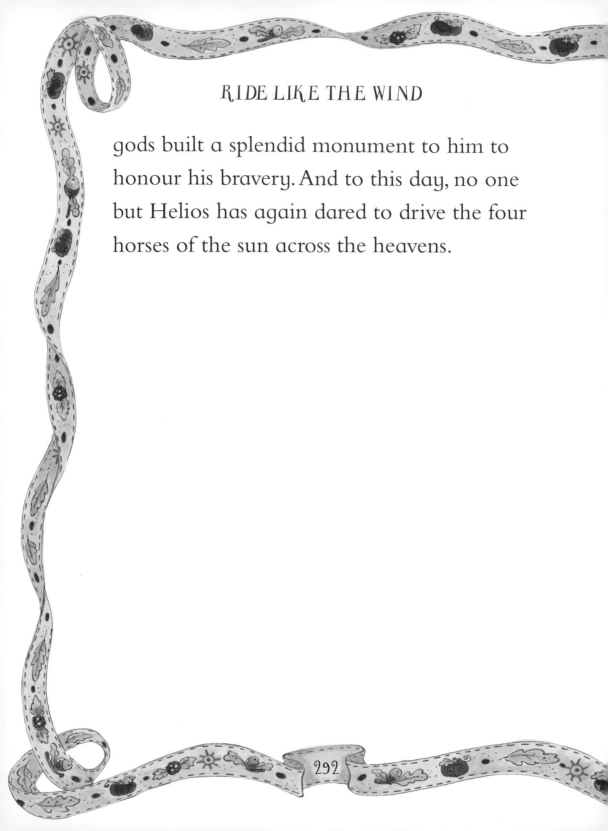

gods built a splendid monument to him to honour his bravery. And to this day, no one but Helios has again dared to drive the four horses of the sun across the heavens.

The Dragon, the Witch and the Twin Horses

An extract from *The Nine Peahens and the Golden Apples* by Andrew Lang

THERE WAS ONCE a prince who fell in love with a beautiful maiden who ruled over a whole empire. The couple were married and went to live in the empress's castle. They were very happy there – and would have no doubt been happy ever after

one of its scales, and dropped it carefully back into the water.

Further down the road, he came upon a fox caught in a trap.

"Oh, my brother," called the fox, "free me from this trap and I will help you when you are in need. Pull out one of my hairs, and when you are in danger twist it in your fingers, and I will come."

So the prince unfastened the trap, pulled out one of the fox's hairs and continued his long journey.

As he was going over the mountain he passed a wolf entangled in a snare.

"Deliver me, brother," the wolf said, "and you will never be sorry for it. Take a lock of my fur, and when you need me twist it in

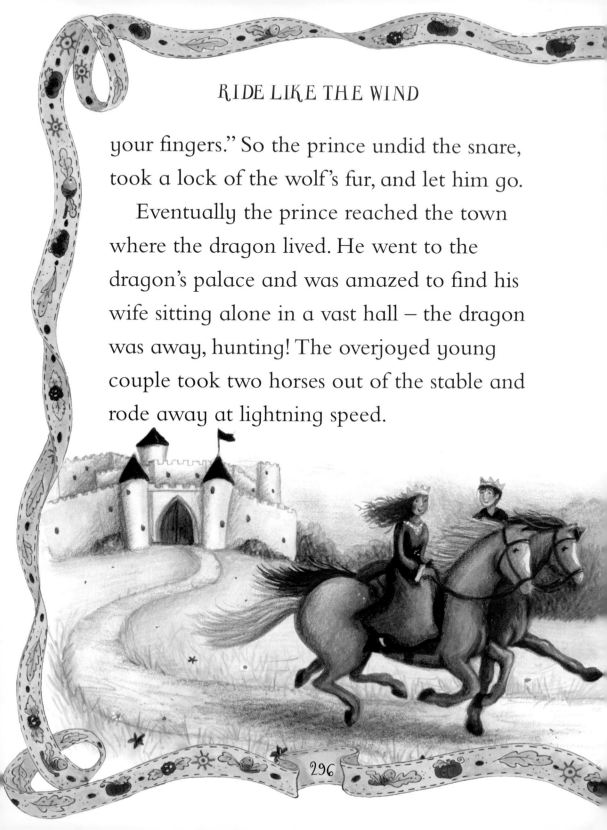

your fingers." So the prince undid the snare, took a lock of the wolf's fur, and let him go.

Eventually the prince reached the town where the dragon lived. He went to the dragon's palace and was amazed to find his wife sitting alone in a vast hall – the dragon was away, hunting! The overjoyed young couple took two horses out of the stable and rode away at lightning speed.

The Dragon, the Witch and the Twin Horses

But soon afterwards the dragon came home and found his prisoner had escaped! He sent at once for his magical horse. It was huge – and it could talk! The dragon said to the horse, "Give me your advice. What shall I do – have my supper as usual, or go after them?"

"Eat your supper first," answered the horse, "then follow them."

So the dragon ate till he could eat no more, then he mounted his horse and set off. In no time at all he had caught up with the escaping couple, snatched the empress out of her saddle and soared off with her, back to his palace.

The grief-stricken prince trudged sadly back to the palace to try again. By the time

he reached it, the dragon had once again
gone hunting, leaving the empress sitting
alone. Quickly, the couple thought of
another escape plan.

The prince dashed away to hide and,
when the dragon came home, the empress
sat down near him and began to flatter
him. At last she said, "But tell me about that
wonderful horse you were riding yesterday.
Surely there isn't another one like it
anywhere in the whole world."

And the dragon answered, "On the top of
a high mountain dwells an old woman,
who has in her stables twelve beautiful
horses and a thin, wretched-looking animal.
This horse is actually the best of the lot. He
is twin brother to my own horse, and can

fly just as high and as fast."

The next day the empress waited till the dragon went out hunting, then ran to where her prince was hiding. She told him all that she had learned and the prince at once hurried off to seek the old woman on the top of the mountain.

At last he found her and, with a bow, he began, "Good greetings to you! I wish to know how I may win one of your horses."

And the old woman said, "If you can take care of my prize mare and her foal for three days, I will give you any horse you like, but if you let them stray you will lose your head."

The prince agreed and strode away to find the mare in the witch's stable.

RIDE LIKE THE WIND

He groomed and fed them and sat up keeping watch. But at length he grew so weary that he fell fast asleep. When he woke he jumped up in terror, for the mare and her foal was nowhere to be seen. So he took the mare's halter and strode off, with a beating heart, over the fields in search of them. Where had they gone?

He had gone some way when he came to a little river. Hastily, he drew the fish scale from his pocket and the fish appeared in the stream beside him, saying, "The witch's mare has changed herself into a big fish, and her foal into a little one. But strike the water with the halter and say, 'Come here, O mare of the mountain witch!' and she will come."

The prince did as he was told and in an instant the mare and her foal stood before him. Then he put the halter round the mare's neck and rode her home, the foal trotting behind them. The old woman was at the door to receive them and gave the prince some food while she led the mare back to the stable.

Next evening, again the prince sat up keeping watch over the mare and her foal, and again sleep overtook him. When he woke up he gave a cry of dismay and leaped off in search of the wanderers. As he went, he drew out the fox hair and twisted it in his fingers. The fox instantly appeared before him and said, "The witch's mare is with us. She has changed herself into a big fox, and her foal into a little one, but strike the ground with the halter and say, 'Come here, O mare of the mountain witch!' and you will see her again."

The prince did so, and in a moment the mare stood before him, with the little foal at her heels. He rode the mare back, and once more the old woman placed food on the table and led the mare back to the stable.

The third night the prince tried even harder to keep awake, but it was of no use. In the morning, the mare and foal were again gone. He started off over the fields in search and pulled out the wolf's grey lock.

There was the wolf, standing before him.

"The witch's mare is with us," answered the wolf. "She has changed herself into a

she-wolf and the foal into a cub. Strike the earth here with the halter, and cry, 'Come to me, O mare of the mountain witch.'"

The prince did as he was bid and there was the mare, with the foal beside her. And when he had ridden her home the old woman was on the steps to receive them, and she set some food before the prince, but led the mare back to her stable.

When the old woman returned to her hut, the prince was at the door waiting.

"I have served you well," said he, "and now for my reward. I want your half-starved horse, for I prefer him to all your other beautiful animals."

"You can't really mean what you say!" replied the witch.

"Yes, I do," said the prince, and the old woman was forced to let him have his way.

So he took leave of her, and put the halter round his horse's neck and led him into the forest. There, he rubbed him down till his skin was shining like gold. And the witch's horse was delighted that he had been chosen by the noble prince, who was so kind and good. The prince mounted his new steed, and the horse flew as fast as he could through the air straight to the dragon's palace.

The empress had been waiting for her prince night and day. She ran out to meet him and he swung her on to his saddle and the horse flew off again.

Not long afterwards the dragon came home and, when he found the empress was missing, he said to his horse, "What shall we do? Shall we eat and drink, or shall we follow the runaways?"

And the horse replied, "It doesn't matter whether you eat or drink now, for you can't catch them."

The furious dragon made no reply to the horse's words, but sprang on its back and set off in a fast chase. And when the couple saw him coming they were frightened and urged the prince's horse faster and faster, till he said, "Fear nothing. No harm can come to us," and their hearts grew calm, for they trusted him.

Soon the dragon's horse was heard panting behind, and he cried out, "Oh, my brother, do not go so fast! I shall sink to the earth if I try to keep up with you."

And the prince's horse answered, "Why do you serve a monster like that? Kick him off, let him break in pieces on the ground, and come and join us."

The dragon's horse agreed with his brother, plunging and rearing, until the dragon fell down to the ground. They saw the monster hit the rocks and break to pieces. The dragon's horse was freed at last and gladly joined his brother, the witch's horse, in serving the noble prince and empress. They all rode back, rejoicing, to the empress's kingdom, where they lived happily for many years.

ADVENTURES ON HORSEBACK

Ciccu and his Helpful Horse

Based on a traditional tale from the
Italian island of Sicily by Andrew Lang

NCE UPON A TIME there lived a man
who had three sons. The eldest was
called Peppe, the second Alfin, and the
youngest Ciccu. They were all very poor
and scraped a living by chopping firewood.

One day the father suddenly fell ill and died, only leaving his sons their little house and the fig tree which grew over it. The brothers buried their father, whom they loved, weeping bitterly. Then they had to get on with earning a living. But without their father, things seemed to go from bad to worse.

Eventually, the brothers didn't even have enough to eat. In desperation, Ciccu went to see if he could find work as a servant in the king's palace. He took with him a basketful of the sweet figs from their father's fig tree. The king thought that the figs were the most delicious he had ever tasted! He gave Ciccu a job and the lad rapidly became one of his favourite servants.

Peppe and Alfin heard that Ciccu had become quite an important person at the palace and grew jealous – so jealous that they thought up a wicked plan to put him to shame. The two brothers came to the king and said to him, "Your Majesty, your palace is beautiful indeed, but to be worthy of you it lacks one thing – the sword of the Man-eater."

"How can I get it?" asked the king.

"Oh, Ciccu can get it for you," they said, "ask him."

So the king sent for Ciccu and said to him, "Ciccu, you must get me the sword of the Man-eater."

Ciccu was very surprised. He walked thoughtfully away to the royal stables and began to stroke his favourite horse, saying, sadly, "We must bid each other goodbye, for the king has sent me away to get the sword of the Man-eater and I will surely die."

Then the horse said, "Fear nothing, and do as I tell you. Beg the king to give you fifty gold pieces and permission to ride me, and the rest will be easy."

Ciccu did what the horse said and the two friends set out, the horse telling Ciccu which way to go.

It took them many days' hard riding before they reached the country where the Man-eater lived. Then the horse told Ciccu to collect a number of mosquitos and tie them up in a bag. When the bag was full Ciccu stole into the house of the Man-eater

(who had gone to hunt for his dinner) and let the mosquitos out in his bedroom. He himself hid carefully under the bed and waited for the Man-eater to return.

The Man-eater came in late. He was very tired so he flung himself on the bed, placing his sword with its shining blade by his side. The mosquitos began to buzz and bite him, and he rolled from side to side trying to catch them.

He was so busy over the mosquitos that he did not hear Ciccu steal softly out of the room with the sword. But the horse heard and stood ready at the door, and as Ciccu came flying down the stairs and jumped on his back he sped away like the wind to the king's palace.

The king had felt very guilty while Ciccu was away, thinking that if the Man-eater ate him, it would be all his fault. He was overjoyed to have him home safe!

But the two brothers were still very jealous, and they said to the king, "It is all very well for Ciccu to have got the sword, but it would have won Your Majesty even more glory if he had actually captured the Man-eater himself."

So the king said, "Ciccu, I shall never rest until you bring me the Man-eater himself."

Ciccu felt very downcast at these words and went to the stable to ask advice of his friend the horse.

"Fear nothing," said the horse, "just say you want me and fifty pieces of gold."

Ciccu did as he was told and the two set out to the country of the Man-eater once more. Ciccu did just as the horse instructed – he bought an axe and a saw, cut down a pine tree in the nearest wood, and started to saw it into planks.

"What are you doing in my wood?"

asked the Man-eater, coming up to them.

"Noble lord," answered Ciccu, "I am making a coffin for the body of Ciccu, who is dead."

"What good news!" answered the Man-eater, who of course did not know whom he was talking to. "Perhaps I can help you," and they set to work sawing and fitting, and very soon the coffin was finished.

Then Ciccu scratched his ear thoughtfully, and cried, "Idiot that I am! I never took any measurements. How am I to know if it is big enough? But now I come to think of it, Ciccu was about your size. I wonder if you would help me by putting yourself in the coffin, and seeing if there is enough room."

"Oh, I'd be delighted!" said the Man-
eater, and he laid himself at full length in
the coffin.

Straight away Ciccu clapped on the lid,
put a strong cord round it, tied it fast to his

horse, and rode back to the king – who was absolutely delighted!

Soon afterwards, the king thought that he should like to get married. He sought everywhere, but he did not hear of any princess that took his fancy. Then the two envious brothers came to him and said, "O King! Ask Ciccu to bring the fairest in the whole world to be your wife."

Now the king had got so used to depending on Ciccu, that he really believed he could do everything. But the mission seemed to Ciccu a hundred times worse than either of the others and, with tears in his eyes, he took his way to the stables.

"Cheer up," laughed the horse, "tell the king you need some bread and honey, and a purse of gold, and leave the rest to me."

Ciccu did as he was told and they started at a gallop. At length they came to the castle where the fairest in the world lived with her parents.

Then said the horse, "You must get down and sit upon that stone, for I must enter the castle alone. As soon as you see me come tearing by with the princess on my back, jump up behind, and hold her tight, so that she does not escape you."

Ciccu seated himself on the stone and the horse went on to the courtyard of the castle, where he began to trot round in a graceful and elegant manner. Soon a crowd collected first to watch him and then to pat him, and the king and queen and princess came with the rest. The eyes of the fairest in the world brightened as she looked, and she sprang on the horse's saddle, crying, "Oh, I really must ride him a little!"

Then the horse made one bound forwards so that the princess was forced to hold on tight to his mane. And as they dashed past the stone where Ciccu was waiting for them, he swung himself up and held her round the waist. Then they sped off, as fast as the wind.

The king of Ciccu's country was watching for them from the top of a tower and, when he saw in the distance a cloud of dust, he ran down to the steps so as to be ready to receive them. Bowing low before the fairest in the world, he spoke, "Noble lady, will you do me the honour of becoming my wife?"

But she answered, "I will only marry you if Ciccu jumps into an oven for three days and three nights."

The king quickly forgot how Ciccu had served him and told him to do as the princess had said.

This time Ciccu felt that no escape was possible and he went to the horse and laid his hand on his neck. "Now it is indeed goodbye, and there is no help to be got even from you," and he told him what fate awaited him.

But the horse said, "Oh, never lose heart, but jump on my back, and ride me till the foam flies in flecks all about me. Then get

down, and scrape off the foam with a knife.
Rub the foam all over you and, when you
are quite covered, you may suffer yourself
to be cast into the oven, for the fire will not
hurt you, nor anything else."

So Ciccu did exactly as the horse told
him. He went back to the king, and before
the eyes of the fairest in the world he sprang
into the oven.

And when the fairest in the world saw
what he had done, love entered into her
heart, and she said to the king, "One thing
more – before I can be your wife, you must
jump into the oven as Ciccu has done."

"Willingly," replied the king, whose head
was full of the princess. He carefully opened
the oven door and sat in the opening,

preparing to get in. But in only a couple of seconds, the flames caught his bottom! He sprang up, howling, and ran off with his breeches on fire, never to be seen again!

Then the fairest in the world held out her hand to Ciccu and smiled, saying, "Now we will be man and wife." So Ciccu married the fairest in the world and his helpful horse was guest of honour at the royal wedding.

Washed Away

From *The Pony Rider Boys in Montana*
by Frank Gee Patchin

In this extract from The Pony Rider Boys, *Walter, Tad,
Ned and Chunky (whose real name is Stacy) go on an adventure
among the mountains of Montana. They are accompanied by
Walter's private tutor, Professor Zeppelin.*

THEY HAD MADE CAMP at sunset on
the banks of Fennell's Creek, a broad,
deep stream that flowed into the clear
waters of the Yellowstone River. Here they
had cooked their supper after many

attempts and much laughter. Later they had rolled themselves into their blankets and gone to sleep.

They had been awakened by Stacy Brown's snoring. They all took the interruption good-naturedly, apart from Ned Rector. He kicked Chunky awake and pounced on him — but Chunky rolled quickly out of the way, leaving Ned scrabbling in the dirt.

"Here, here!" scolded the professor. "Stop this nonsense. I want to go to sleep. Into your blankets, every one of you."

It was doubtful that the boys even heard his voice, so absorbed were they in the mad scramble of Ned Rector after the rolling Stacy Brown.

The ponies, disturbed by the noise and excitement, had sprung to their feet and were moving about restlessly in the bushes where they were tethered.

"Look out for the river!" warned Tad, suddenly remembering that they were camping right on the riverbank.

But just then, Stacy cried, "Help, help! I'm rolling in!" He grasped frantically at weeds as he rolled down the almost vertical bank and, with a mighty splash, he plunged into the stream.

"He's in!" cried Walter.

With a warning cry to the others to bring lights, Tad, without an instant's hesitation, leaped over the edge and went shooting down it on his bottom.

"Tad's gone in, too," shouted Walter excitedly, as their ears caught a second loud splash.

Ned Rector stood as if dazed.

"They're in the river! Don't you understand?" cried Walter sharply, moving forwards as if to follow over the bank in an effort to rescue his companions.

"Keep back!" commanded the professor. "You'll all drown if you go over that bank. Use your eyes! Do you see them?" He peered down anxiously into the shadows.

"No!" shouted Ned.

Down the stream a short distance they could hear water roaring over the rocks, from where it dropped some twenty feet and continued on its course. The falls there were known as Buttermilk Falls, because of the churning the water received in its lively drop, and more than one mountaineer had been swept over them to his death in times of high water.

Between the camp and these falls there was a sharp bend in the river and the boys reckoned their companions had undoubtedly been swept around the bend and out of sight.

"They have gone downstream," answered

the professor shortly. "Run for it, boys!
Run as you never ran before!"

Ned dived for the thicket
where the ponies were
tethered. It was the work of
a moment only to release
Bad-eye. Saddling
him in lightning
speed, Ned threw
himself upon the
surprised animal's
back and, with a
wild yell, sent the broncho plunging
through the camp. He was nearly unseated
when Bad-eye suddenly veered to avoid
stepping onto the camp fire.

The lad gripped the pony's mane and

hung on desperately until he finally succeeded in righting himself, all the while kicking the pony's sides with his bare feet to urge him on faster.

They were out of the camp, tearing through the thicket before the professor and Walter had even got beyond the glow of the fire. They swung round the river bend at a tremendous pace. Ned was able to see little about him. "Tad! Chunky!" he shouted.

A faint call answered him. He was not quite sure that it was not an echo of his own voice. "Hurry!" It seemed a long distance away – that faint reply to his hail.

"That you, Tad?"

"Y-e-s."

"Where are you? I don't see you."

"In the river. Just below the bend. I am holding to a rock. It's awful slippery and I'm freezing too."

"All right. Is Stacy with you?"

"Yes, I've got him."

"Good! Have courage! I'll be with you," said Ned encouragingly.

"You'll have to hurry. I can't hold on much longer – and the falls are just below me here."

Ned had no need to be told that. The roar of the falls was loud in his ears and he could almost feel the spray on his face.

Ned was off like a shot on Bad-eye, back up river to where Professor Zepplin and Walter were running to catch up with him.

"Got a rope?" he shouted.

"No," answered Walter.

"Then get one and hurry around the bend. You'll be needed there in a minute. I'm going into the stream."

Then, without an instant's hesitation, Ned Rector set his pony towards the bank and urged him forwards. Every moment was precious now.

"Stop! I forbid it!" thundered the professor.

Ned paid no attention to him. "Just hurry with that rope!" he commanded. Then "Hi-yi!" the Pony Rider exclaimed, loudly, bringing the reins down smartly onto Bad-eye.

With a squeal the little animal plunged over the bank. The treacherous sands gave way beneath his feet and the pony landed clumsily. Ned was hurled from the saddle but clung doggedly to the bridle reins. The pony floundered down the slippery bank, then entered the water with a mighty splash. Ned could have screamed from the shock of the icy water!

While Bad-eye's flying hoofs beat the water almost into a froth, Ned exerted all his strength to swim out further towards the middle of the stream, keeping a firm grip on the reins. Then the pony righted himself and instinctively began swimming towards the bank.

"No!" Ned gasped, and he urged the pony back into the current. Under the strong guiding hand of his master, the

animal began swimming downstream.

"I'm coming!" shouted Ned. "I'm coming!" he repeated, as they swung around the wide sweeping curve. "Are you there, Tad?"

"Yes," was the scarcely distinguishable reply. "But I've got to let go."

"You hold on. Bad-eye and I will be there in a minute and the professor is hurrying down along the bank with a rope for you."

"I'm all numb, that's the trouble," answered Tad weakly.

Ned knew that the plucky lad was near-enough exhausted. He swam the pony alongside them, pulling hard on the reins to slow the animal down.

"Is Chunky able to help himself?"

"Yes, just."

"Then both of you grab Bad-eye by the mane as he goes by. Don't you miss, for if you do, we're all lost."

The next moment Tad, still clinging to Chunky, fastened his right hand in the broncho's mane. All three of the boys were now clinging to the brave animal.

Ned jumped off and trod water alongside the pony, for he realized that they had dropped back a few feet after taking on the extra weight.

"Work further back and get hold of the saddle," Ned directed.

Tad followed his instructions.

"I'm afraid he'll never make it with all of

us," groaned Ned. But at that instant his hand hit a hard, cold object. It was the slender, pillar-like rock that Tad had been clinging to for so long in the icy water. Ned cast loose from Bad-eye and threw both arms about the rock.

The pony, freed from a share of his burden, struck off upstream against the current, making excellent headway back to camp.

"I don't like to do this," Tad called back.

337

"I wouldn't, were it not for Chunky. He couldn't have stood it there another minute."

"Professor, are you there?" Ned yelled upwards as the pony struck out with the two boys for the shore.

"Yes!" came the out-of-breath reply. "That was a very brave thing to do, Master Ned. Very brave."

"Thank you, Professor. Now cast that rope to me. I'm afraid I shall never be able to hold on here alone as long as Tad did. B-r-r-r, but it's cold!" he shivered.

The professor tried his hand at casting the rope, but he didn't get it anywhere near Ned, who was starting to struggle.

The professor tried again… and again…

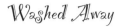

but it was still no good.

Ned had been hanging on for a good ten minutes by now, and feared he could hang on no longer when he heard someone shouting cheerily up the stream. Why, it was Tad Butler!

The minute that Bad-eye had reached the shore, Tad had seen Walter saddling Pink-eye. Tad had mounted the pony and led him into the water. He was now returning to rescue his brave friend, unwilling to trust the perilous trip to anyone else.

"I was afraid Walt would go over the falls, pony and all," Tad explained, wheeling alongside Ned and picking him up from the rock. "When we get ashore, I'll race you back to camp," he laughed.

"You're on," answered Ned promptly. "And the one who loses has to cook the breakfast."

The Giant and the Unicorn

A retelling of a traditional Jewish
folktale by Gertrude Landa

ALL THE ANIMALS gathered in front
of the Ark and began to march
forwards into it, while Father Noah
carefully inspected them. He seemed very
troubled indeed. "I wonder," he said to
himself, "how I shall obtain a unicorn,

and how I shall get it into the Ark."

"I can bring you a unicorn, Father Noah," he heard in a booming voice of thunder, and turning round he saw the giant, Og. "But you must agree to save me from the flood as well."

"Go away," cried Noah. "You are not an animal – giants aren't allowed on the Ark."

"Please pity me," whined the giant to Noah. "See how I am shrinking. Once I was so tall that I could drink water from the clouds and warm my face at the sun. I fear not that I shall be drowned, but that all the food will be destroyed and that I shall perish of hunger."

Noah refused once more and Og wandered off. But he was soon back, bringing with him a unicorn.

It was huge, although the giant said it was the smallest he could find. It lay down in front of the Ark, and for some time Noah was puzzled about what to do, until at last a bright idea struck him. He attached the huge beast to the Ark by a rope fastened to its horn so that it could swim alongside them and be fed.

Og seated himself on a mountain nearby and watched the rain pouring down. It fell faster and faster in torrents until the rivers overflowed and the waters began to rise rapidly on the land and sweep all things away. Father Noah stood gloomily before the door of the Ark until the water reached his neck. Then it swept him inside. The door closed with a bang, and the Ark rose gallantly on the flood and began to move along. The unicorn swam alongside and, as it passed Og, the giant jumped nimbly on to its back.

"See, Father Noah," he cried, with a huge chuckle, "you will have to save me after all, or I will snatch all the food you put through the window for the unicorn."

Noah saw that it was useless to argue with Og, who might easily, indeed, sink the Ark with his tremendous strength.

"I will make a bargain with you," Noah shouted from a window. "I will feed you, but you must promise to be a servant for me and my family when the flood is over."

Og was very hungry, so he accepted the

conditions and devoured his first breakfast.

The rain continued to fall in great big sheets that shut out the light of day. Inside the Ark, however, all was bright and cheerful, for Noah had placed precious stones in the windows.

One day the rain ceased, the clouds rolled away and the sun shone brilliantly again. How strange the world looked! It was like a vast ocean. Nothing but water could be seen anywhere, and only one or two of the highest mountain-tops peeped above the flood. All the world was drowned, and Noah gazed on the desolate scene from one of the windows with tears in his eyes.

Finally, after sailing for days and days some land appeared and the Ark rested on

Mount Ararat. Og sat nearby on the hillside and watched the animals leave the Ark and spread out over the land. Finally Noah set loose the mighty unicorn and it galloped away and disappeared from sight.

Then Noah's children began to build houses – and Og had to labour as their servant. Daily he complained that he was shrinking to the size of the mortals, for Noah said there was not enough food for him to keep his size.

And that is how giants came to be no different from humans and how the unicorn became the rarest beast of all.

A Stormy Day

From *Black Beauty* by Anna Sewell

In this extract from the famous Victorian novel, Black Beauty is a young horse owned by a good, animal-loving master called Squire Gordon. Here, he repays his master's kindness...

ONE DAY LATE in the autumn my master had to go on a long journey for business. I was put into the dog-cart and the coachman, John, drove it for my master. I always liked to go in the dog-cart, it was so light and the high wheels ran along so

pleasantly. The wind was high and it blew
the leaves across the road in a shower. There
had been a great deal of rain. Many of the
meadows were under water and in one part
of the low road the water was halfway up
to my knees – but the bottom was level and
my master drove gently, so it was no matter.

We went along till we came to the toll-
gate and the low wooden bridge. The river
was rather high, and in the middle of the
bridge the water was nearly up to the
woodwork and planks. There were
substantial rails on each side, however, so
people did not mind it. The man at the gate
said he feared it would be a bad night.

We got to the town and I had a good
feed from a nosebag while the master went

about his business. He was engaged a long time, so we did not start for home till rather late in the afternoon. The wind was then much higher and I heard the master say to John that he had never been out in such a storm. I thought so too, as we went along the skirts of a wood, where the great branches were swaying about like twigs and the rushing sound was terrible.

"I wish we were well out of this wood," said my master.

"Yes, sir," said John, "it would be rather awkward if one of these branches came down upon us."

The words were scarcely out of his mouth when there was a groan and a crack and a splitting sound, and crashing down

among the other trees came an oak, torn up
by the roots. It fell right across the road just
before us. I will never say I was not
frightened, for I was. I reared up, and I

believe I trembled, but I did not turn around or run away – I was not brought up to behave like that. John jumped out and was in a moment at my head.

"That was a very close call," said my master. "What's to be done now?"

"Well, sir, we can't drive over that tree, nor can we get around it. We'll have to go back to the crossroads, I'm afraid. We are a good six miles away from the wooden bridge, so we'll be home late, but the horse is doing fine."

So back we went to the crossroads. By the time we got to the bridge it was very nearly dark. We could just see that the water was over the middle of it, but as that happened sometimes when the floods were

out, master did not stop.

We were going along at a good pace, but the moment my feet touched the first part of the bridge I felt sure there was something wrong. I dare not go forwards and I made a dead stop.

"Go on, Beauty," said my master, and he gave me a touch with the whip, but I dared not stir. He gave me another touch and I jumped, but I dared not go forwards.

"There's something wrong, sir," said John, and he sprang out of the dog-cart, came to my head and looked all about. He tried to lead me forwards.

"Come on, Beauty, what's the matter?" Of course I could not tell him, but I knew very well that the bridge was not safe.

Just then the man at the toll-gate on the other side ran out of the house waving his hands around like a mad person.

"Hoy, hoy, hoy! Halloo! Stop!" he cried.

"What's the matter?" shouted my master anxiously.

"The bridge is broken in the middle and part of it is carried away, if you ride onto it you'll be into the river for sure."

"Thank goodness we didn't!" cried my master loudly.

"You Beauty!" said John, and he took the bridle and gently turned me round to the righthand road by the riverside.

The sun had been set for some time and the wind seemed to have lulled off after the furious blast that tore up the tree. It grew darker and darker, stiller and stiller.

I trotted quietly along, the wheels hardly making a sound on the soft road. For a good while neither my master nor John spoke, and then my master began talking in a serious voice.

They thought that if I had gone on as my master had wanted me to, the bridge would have most likely given way under us, and horse, chaise, master and man would have fallen into the river. As the current was flowing very strongly, and there was no light and no help at hand, it was more than likely we would have all have drowned.

My master said that God had given men reason by which they could find out things for themselves, but he had given animals knowledge that did not depend on reason, and that this was sometimes better, and they had often used this to save the lives of people. John had many stories to tell of

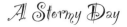

horses and dogs and the wonderful things they had done.

At last we came to the park gates and found the gardener looking out for us. He said that my mistress had been in a dreadful state ever since dark, as she feared some accident had happened. We saw a light at the hall-door and at the upper windows, and as we came up she ran out outside, saying, "Are you really safe, my dear? Oh! I have been so anxious, fancying all sorts of terrible things."

And my master replied, "If Black Beauty had not been wiser than us, then we would have all have been carried down the river at the wooden bridge."

I heard no more, as they went into the

house and John took me to the stable. Oh, what a good supper he gave me that night, a good bran mash and some crushed beans with my oats, and such a thick bed of straw! And I was glad of it, for I was tired.

The Brave Horse Brothers

A version of an ancient Romanian
folktale by Andrew Lang

ONCE UPON A TIME there lived an
emperor who was a great conqueror,
and he reigned over more countries than
anyone else in the world. Whenever he
invaded a kingdom, he only granted peace

on the condition that the king should send one of his sons to him for ten years' service.

One old king had stood against the emperor for many years. But now he was old and worn-out and had no choice but to accept the emperor as his overlord. However he had no son to send, only three daughters.

"I will go," urged the eldest girl, despite her father's protests that it was too dangerous for her.

So she put on a coat of golden armour, chose the most spirited jet-black horse in the royal stables, and darted away.

However, unbeknown to his daughters, the old king was a magician. He overtook the eldest princess, changed himself into a wolf, and lay down under a bridge he knew she would have to cross.

After about half an hour his daughter arrived at the bridge. With a deep growl, the wolf sprang up onto the bridge in front of the princess. The wolf was so terrifying that the princess turned her horse around at

once and galloped full out until she saw the gates of the palace.

The very next day, the second princess begged to go instead. She donned gleaming silver armour and chose a prancing white stallion. But although she was prepared for the appearance of the wolf when she reached the bridge, she was just as terrified and galloped home as fast as her horse could carry her.

The following morning, the youngest princess made her preparations to go to the emperor. She went to the royal stables to choose a horse and saw her father's old war-horse stretched sadly out on the straw. The horse lifted his head and said softly, "Ah, what a warrior your father was and what good times we shared together! But now I too have grown old, and my master has forgotten me. Yet, it is not too late, and if I were properly tended, in a week I could better any horse in the stables!"

"And how should you be tended?" asked the girl.

"For a week, I must be rubbed down morning and evening with rainwater, my barley must be boiled in milk, and my feet must be washed in oil."

"I should like to try the treatment, as you might help me in carrying out my scheme."

"Try it then, mistress, and I promise you won't be sorry."

So the princess did as the horse had said and in a week's time it woke up one morning to find its skin shining like a mirror, its body as fat as a watermelon and its movement as light as a deer.

Then, looking at the princess who had come early to the stable, the horse said joyfully, "May success always be yours, for you have given me back my life. I shall serve you as I served your father, if you will only listen to what I say."

And so the delighted youngest daughter dressed in boy's clothes and rode away on the old war-horse.

A day's journey from the palace, she reached the bridge. But before they came in sight of it, the horse spoke soothing words and urged her not to be frightened. The huge wolf bounded howling towards her, but neither the horse nor the princess flinched. Instead, the princess bravely wielded her sword and the horse charged forwards across the bridge, so that the wolf shrank back in fear.

Once safely on the other side, the horse informed the princess that the wolf was really her own father! The girl didn't believe him – until the wolf changed back into her father before her very eyes.

The king flung his arms round her, saying, "Now I see that you are as brave as the bravest and as wise as the wisest, for you have chosen the right horse. With his help, you may reach the emperor and do well." Then the princess received his blessing and they went their different ways.

The princess rode on until she came to the mountains that hold up the roof of the world. There she met two genies who had been fighting fiercely for years.

Seeing what they took to be a young man, one of the genies called out, "Deliver me from my enemy and I will give you a magic horn of power," while the other cried, "Help me to conquer this thief and you shall have my horse, Sunlight."

Before answering, the princess asked her own horse which offer she should accept.

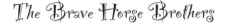

He advised her to side with the genie who
was master of Sunlight – for Sunlight was
his own younger brother and even faster
and stronger than himself.

So the princess fought the other genie
until he begged for mercy. The genie who
was left victorious asked the princess to
come back with him to his house so he
could hand over Sunlight, as he had
promised he would.

The winning genie's mother was
overjoyed to see her son return safe and
sound. However, she was a very cunning
woman who at once suspected that the boy
who had come to the rescue of her son was
a girl in disguise!

She told the genie that she would make

the perfect wife for him. The genie scoffed, so to prove what she had said, at night, she laid on each of their pillows a handful of magic flowers that fade at the touch of a man, but remain eternally fresh in the fingers of a woman.

This was very clever of the genie's mother, but the horse warned the princess what to expect. So when the house was silent, she stole very softly to the genie's room and exchanged his faded flowers for those she held.

At the break of day, the old woman ran to see her son and found, as she knew she would, a bunch of dead flowers in his hand. But when she came to the bedside of the still-sleeping princess, she was astonished to

see her also grasping withered flowers.

There was nothing for the mother to do but submit, and when the princess awoke, she rode off on Sunlight.

Before they had got very far, the old war-horse, who was galloping at her side, said, "Mistress, I am old and now there is someone to take my place. Give me leave, therefore, to return home, and continue your journey under the care of my brother. Put your faith in him as you put it in me, and you will never be sorry."

Then, with tears in her eyes, the princess took leave of her old horse, who galloped back to her father.

She had ridden only a few miles further, when she saw a long golden curl lying on the road before her. She asked Sunlight whether it would be better to take it or leave it there.

"Take it," said Sunlight, "and you won't be sorry."

At this the girl dismounted and, picking up the curl, wound it round her neck to keep it safe.

At length they reached the court of the emperor. He was sitting on his throne, surrounded by the sons of the other kings, who served him as pages. The princess explained why she had come and the emperor received her kindly, declaring himself fortunate at finding a new page that was so brave, but also so charming.

From that moment on, the princess was

the emperor's new favourite. The other
pages soon grew jealous, and thought up a
wicked plan to get rid of the new prince.
They told the emperor that their new
companion had boasted that he knew
where the beautiful lost princess, Iliane, was
to be found – and that he had a curl of her
hair in his possession.

The emperor commanded his favourite
page to be brought before him at once and
said, "You have hidden from me the fact
that you knew the golden-haired Iliane!
Why did you do this, for I have treated you
more kindly than all my other pages? Listen
to me – unless you bring me the owner of
this lock of hair, I will have your head cut
off. Now go!"

Bowing low, the princess sadly left his presence and went to consult Sunlight. At the horse's first words she brightened up – Sunlight had a plan!

"Do not be afraid, mistress, it is indeed Iliane's hair that you picked up on the road. A genie carried her off, but she is quite safe on a far-off island. Go back to the emperor and ask him for twenty ships filled with precious merchandise with which to tempt Iliane on board."

The ships were soon ready and the youngest princess entered the largest and finest, with Sunlight at her side. Then the sails were spread and the voyage began.

For seven weeks the wind blew them straight towards the west, until early one

morning they caught sight of the island.

They cast anchor in a little bay and the princess disembarked with Sunlight. She tied a pair of tiny gold slippers to her belt, as the horse advised her to do.

Then, mounting Sunlight, she rode until she met three servants. Their greedy eyes were caught by the glistening gold of the slippers and they hastened to their mistress to tell her of the arrival of the ships.

Luckily the genie was away, so for the moment Iliane was free and alone. The servants described the slippers to her so well that she insisted on going to see them for herself straightaway, and she rushed off to the see them.

The slippers were even lovelier than she expected and so when the youngest princess begged Iliane to come onto the ships and inspect the other precious things, Iliane's curiosity was too great to refuse and she went onboard.

Iliane was so busy looking at all the merchandise that she didn't even notice that the ship started moving, and soon they were flying along with the wind behind them.

Thus they arrived at the court of the emperor, who received Iliane with all the respect that was due to her and fell in love at first sight.

However, this did not seem to please Iliane. She wondered how it was that, while other girls did as they liked, she was always held captive in someone's power.

As for the youngest princess, she bowed low to the emperor and said, "Mighty Sovereign, all hail! I have fulfilled this impossible task for you."

"I am content," replied the emperor, "and when I am dead it is you who will sit upon my throne – for I have no son."

But though the emperor was satisfied, Iliane was not. She made a secret sign to Sunlight and the horse understood what he was to do.

Sunlight took a deep breath, then from one nostril breathed fresh air all over the youngest princess. To her surprise she was immediately transformed into a handsome young prince!

From the other nostril the horse snorted a burning wind over the emperor, and he shrivelled up where he stood, leaving only a little heap of ashes.

Then Iliane turned to the prince and said, "It is you who brought me here. You saved me from the genie. You shall be my husband. I wish to marry you."

"Yes, I wish to marry you too," said the young prince, with a smile. And they lived happily with Sunlight to a ripe old age.

The Princess on the Glass Hill

A retelling of an ancient Norwegian
fairytale by Sir George Webbe Dasent

ONCE UPON A TIME there was a man
who had a meadow, and in the
meadow there was a hay barn. But for the
last few years there had been very little hay,
because on every St John's night the crop
was eaten down to the very ground. It was

just as if a whole drove of sheep had been there feeding on it overnight. The man grew weary of losing his hay so he told his three sons that one of them must go and sleep in the barn on the next St John's night and stop whatever was happening.

Well, the time came and the eldest son set off to the barn. He lay down to sleep, but there came a loud rumble and an earthquake, and the boy ran home in fear. The hay was eaten up again, just as it had been before.

The next St John's night, the middle son set off to try his luck. But once again there came a terrible earthquake, and he ran away frightened. All the hay was eaten up, just as before.

Next year it was Boots, the youngest brother's turn. The other two laughed at him, saying Boots was useless and would have no more luck than they did.

Boots tooks no notice however, and went to the barn. That night there was an enormous earthquake. The lad thought the walls and roof were coming down on his head, but it soon passed, and all was still about him.

After a little while, he crept to the door and there

outside stood a horse feeding away. So big, and fat, and grand a horse, Boots had never set eyes on! By his side on the grass lay a saddle and bridle, and a full set of armour for a knight, made of gleaming brass.

'Ho, ho,' thought the lad, 'it's you, is it, that eats up our hay? I'll soon put a spoke in your wheel, just see if I don't.'

So Boots threw the saddle and bridle over the horse and it became so tame that the lad could do whatever he liked with it.

So he got on its back and rode off with it to a secret place his brothers knew nothing of, and there he kept the horse.

When he got home, his brothers laughed and asked how he had fared.

"Well," said Boots, "all I can say is, I lay in the barn till the sun rose, and neither saw nor heard anything."

"A pretty story," said his brothers, and they trudged off to the meadow. But when the two reached it, there stood the grass as just as it had been overnight.

Well, the next St John's eve it was the same story over again. Boots went to the barn and everything happened just as it had the year before. This time, the horse that appeared was even finer and fatter than the first. By its side was a saddle and bridle and a full suit of silver armour. Well, the lad tamed and rode this horse, too, and took it to the hiding-place where he kept the first horse, and after that he went home.

"I suppose you'll tell us," said one of his brothers, "there's a fine crop this year too, up in the hayfield."

"Well, so there is," said Boots, and his brothers couldn't believe their eyes when they saw he was telling the truth.

Now, when the third St John's eve came, Boots again went to the barn. The very same thing happened once more – and the horse that appeared was far, far bigger and fatter than the first two, with a saddle, bridle and armour of dazzling gold beside it. The boy again tamed it and rode off with it to the hiding-place where he kept the other two horses.

When he got home, his two brothers made fun of him again and said many spiteful things, but when they went to the field, there stood the grass as fine this time as it had been twice before.

Now, the king of the country where Boots lived had a daughter who was so lovely that anyone who set eyes on her fell head over heels in love. She lived in a palace next to which there was a high, high hill, made entirely of glass, as smooth and slippery as ice.

One day, the king announced that he would give half his kingdom and his daughter's hand in marriage to the man who could ride up to the top of the hill, to where the princess was to sit, and take three golden apples from her lap.

All the princes and knights who heard this came riding to the kingdom from all parts of the world. On the day of the trial, there was such a crowd of princes and knights under the glass hill that it made one's head whirl to look at them. Everyone else in the kingdom came to watch. The two elder brothers set off with the rest, telling Boots he wasn't allowed to go with them, and must stay at home.

Now when the two brothers came to the hill of glass, the knights and princes were all hard at it, riding their horses till they were exhausted. But it was no good, for as soon as the horses set foot on the hill, down they slipped. There wasn't one who could get a yard or two up – and no wonder, for the glass hill was smooth, slippery and very steep. At last all their horses were so weary that the knights had to give up trying.

The king was just thinking to himself that he would proclaim a new trial for the next day, to see if they would have better luck, when all at once a knight came riding up on a brave steed. The knight had brass armour, and the horse a brass bit in his mouth. He rode his horse towards the hill and went up about a third of the way easily, then turned his horse round and rode down again.

The princess thought she had never seen a knight so handsome, so she threw down one of the golden apples after him, and he caught it. But when the knight got to the bottom of the hill he rode off so fast that no one could tell what had become of him.

That evening the two brothers went home and told Boots all about the wondrous knight and his amazing horse. "Oh! I should so like to have seen them," said Boots, who sat by the fireside.

Next day the brothers set off once more and again made Boots stay at home.

When the brothers got to the hill of glass, all the princes and knights were trying to ride up it again. But it was no good – they rode and slipped, just as they had done the day before.

The king was just about to proclaim that there would be one last day of the trial, when a new knight came riding up. His steed was even braver and finer than the

horse ridden by the knight in brass. This knight was wearing silver armour, and his horse had a silver saddle and bridle, all so bright that moonbeams gleamed from it.

The knight rode straight at the hill and went up two-thirds of the way easily, before he wheeled his horse round and rode back down again.

The princess liked him even better than the knight in brass. She threw the second apple after him and he caught it. But after the knight reached the bottom of the hill, he rode off so fast that no one could see what became of him.

That evening the two brothers went home full of news about the incredible knight and his shining horse.

"Oh!" said Boots, "I should so like to have seen them too."

On the third day everything happened as before – Boots begged to go and see the sight, but the two brothers wouldn't hear of it, and told him to stay at home.

When they got to the hill there was no one who could get so much as a yard up it. But at last came a knight riding on a steed so brave and fine that no one had ever seen its match.

The knight was wearing a suit of golden armour, and his horse had a golden saddle and bridle – so bright that sunbeams gleamed from them.

He rode right at the hill and all the way to the top! He took the third golden apple from the princess's lap and then turned his horse and rode down again.

As soon as he got to the bottom, he rode off at full speed and was soon out of sight.

Now, when the two brothers got home, you may guess what they had to say about the knight in golden armour and his dazzling horse!

"Oh," said Boots, "I should so like to have seen them, that I should."

The next day everyone in the kingdom was commanded to come before the king and the princess – but no one showed a golden apple. The two brothers of Boots were the last of all, so the king asked them if there was no one else in the kingdom who hadn't come.

"Oh, yes," said they, "we have a brother, but he didn't carry off the golden apple. He hasn't left home these last three days."

"Never mind that," said the king, "tell him to come, like everyone else."

So Boots went up to the palace.

"How, now," said the king, "have you got a golden apple? Speak out!"

"Yes, I have," said Boots, "here is the first, and here is the second, and here is the third one too!"

And with that he pulled all of the three golden apples out of his pocket! And at the same time he threw off his raggedy clothes and stood before them in the gleaming golden armour.

"Yes!" said the king. "You shall have my

daughter, and half my kingdom – for you well deserve both her and it."

So Boots married the princess and the bridal feast was so merry that the celebrations are still going on today.

The Horses of the Sun Meadow

By Andrew Lang

There are many different versions of this traditional tale, sometimes known as 'The Enchanted Knife'.

ONCE UPON A TIME there lived a young man who vowed to himself that he would only marry a royal. So one day he plucked up all his courage and went to the palace to ask the emperor for his

daughter's hand in marriage. The emperor
wasn't pleased at the thought of such a
match for his child, so he set the lad what
he thought was an impossible task. The
emperor's pride and joy was his royal stable
full of the fine horses – yet he had heard of
three horses that were even finer still, and
longed for these above all other things.

So he said, "Very well, my son, if you can win the princess you shall have her, but the conditions are these – in eight days you must manage to find, tame and bring to me three special wild horses. The first is pure white, the second a foxy-red with a black head, and the third is coal-black with a white head and feet. And on top of all that, you must also bring as a present to the empress, my wife, as much gold as the three horses can carry on their backs."

The young man listened in dismay, and thought he must give in, but with an effort he thanked the emperor for his kindness and left the palace, wondering how he was to fulfil the task.

Luckily for him, the emperor's daughter

had overheard everything her father had said, and peeping through a curtain had seen the youth. She thought him more handsome than anyone she had ever beheld, and so she decided to help him.

She wrote him a letter and gave it to a trustworthy servant to deliver. The letter begged him to meet her early the next day and not to undertake other plans in the meantime.

That night, when her father was fast asleep, the emperor's daughter crept softly into his chamber and took out an enchanted knife from the chest where he kept his treasures.

The sun had hardly risen the following morning when the princess's maid brought the young man to meet her outside her apartments. Neither spoke for some minutes, but stood holding each other's hands. They fell instantly in love with each other, and felt full of joy. After a while they both cried out that nothing but death should part them, and they would do anything to stay together.

So the emperor's daughter gave the young man the enchanted knife, which she had taken from her father.

"Take my horse," she said, "and ride straight through the wood towards the sunset till you come to a hill with three peaks. When you get there, turn first to the right and then to the left, and you will find yourself in a sun meadow, where there are many horses are feeding. Out of these many horses you must pick out the three described to you by my father. If they refuse to let you near, take out this knife, and let the sun shine on it so that the whole meadow is lit up by its rays. The horses will then come to you of their own accord, and will let you lead them away.

"When you have the horses safely in your control, find the cypress tree with brass roots, silver boughs and gold leaves. Go to it, and cut away the roots with your knife, and you will come to countless bags of gold. Load the horses with all they can carry, and return to my father, and tell him that you have done your task, and can now claim me for your wife."

The young man did exactly as the princess instructed. The horse's were drawn to the reflection of the sun in the knife, and came willingly to him. The cypress tree was there too, just as the princess had said.

When the emperor saw the young man with the three horses he marvelled! He

never guessed how the young man had
outsmarted him – and he didn't realize that
his enchanted knife was missing until
after the wedding!

Griffen, the High Flyer

By James Baldwin

The winged horse in this story is a descendant of Pegasus who, according to Greek mythology, carried thunderbolts for the great god Zeus.

O LD ATLANTES, THE WIZARD of the Pyrenees, built a tower for his laboratory on the topmost peak of a grey mountain. He built it with solid walls, a single narrow door, and a dome of glass at the top. By night, he sat in the dome and gazed at the stars. By day, he sat inside the tower surrounded by his magic circles and books and pots and vials and herbs. Sometimes the people in the valley below saw thick clouds of black smoke coming out of the chimney of the wizard's den and even reported that they had seen sheets of flame and balls of red fire shooting out from the high tower.

Everyone in the nearby countryside feared Atlantes, but he didn't care as long as they did not disturb him in his studies and experiments. He was searching for the secret of how to make the magical philosopher's stone, with which he would be able to turn anything into gold.

Atlantes thought that he knew how to make it, if only he could get a vial of lightning…

One night, when a great storm was raging in the mountains, and the thunder was rolling from peak to peak, and flashes of lightning filled the air with terror, Atlantes tried an experiment. He left his tower and went to a cave in the side of the mountain, where he placed a huge jar and several pots of magic ingredients. He arranged them very carefully, and went back to his tower to wait.

In the morning, when the storm had cleared away, the wizard hurried to the cave. To his amazement there sprang from the huge jar a white horse with great wings

that reflected all of the colours of the
rainbow. Atlantes thought he must look very
like Pegasus, the mythical horse. He called
the horse Griffen and the airy creature
became his.

Now the wizard, with the aid of his
winged steed, built himself an even more
marvellous castle of magic, with shining
walls and lofty turrets. The local people
were stunned to look up and see it among
the mountaintops, but even more amazed to
see a horse flying in mid-air with the
white-bearded wizard seated on its back.

Every morning, with his great spectacles
astride his nose and a great big book in his
hands, Atlantes would mount his winged
horse and soar out over the countryside to

some spot where a noble knight or a fair maiden would be likely to be passing during the day.

He would wait until his unsuspecting victim drew near, then the horse would suddenly swoop down and block the road. Then Atlantes would read aloud from his book and the traveller would forget everything, come meekly forwards, allowing themselves to be lifted up behind the wizard and carried aloft on Griffen back to the magic castle, to keep Atlantes company there forever.

Time passed, and so many people went missing from the surrounding lands that a brave young man called Astolpho made up his mind to find the castle and defeat the

wizard. He rode a beautiful black horse named Rabican, which was so sure-footed it could climb where no other horse could.

So Astolpho on Rabican made his way high up the mountain and finally reached the entrance to the great white castle. The gate was open, as if beckoning him to enter. Astolpho urged Rabican forwards into a courtyard with shady trees and fountains. Knights and ladies were there playing chess, but they took no notice of him.

All at once, an old man with a long flowing beard came out of the castle and began to read. But Astolpho too had a book, a book given to him by an Indian prince, which contained spells against all enchantments.

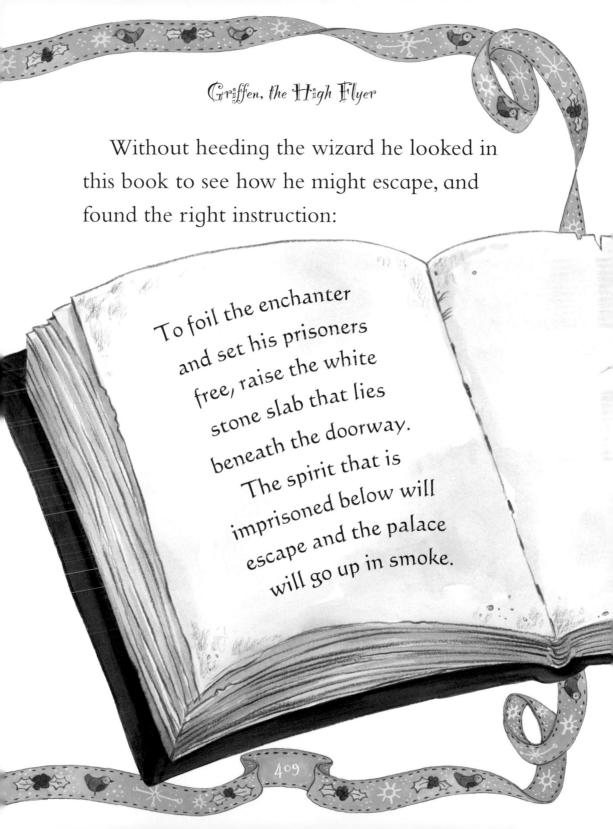

Without heeding the wizard he looked in this book to see how he might escape, and found the right instruction:

To foil the enchanter and set his prisoners free, raise the white stone slab that lies beneath the doorway. The spirit that is imprisoned below will escape and the palace will go up in smoke.

While the wizard was still
trying to complete the words
of his spell, Astolpho slid
from Rabican's back, ran
to the doorway, found the
white stone, and prised it
up with his spear. There,
before him, was a spacious
chamber. Griffen was
inside, saddled and bridled
and ready for flight.
Astolpho lost no time in
springing onto his back and
soaring up into the air.

With a clap of thunder, the
palace of enchantment disappeared,
leaving the knights and ladies standing

dazed on the mountainside.
One by one, they awoke from
the spells placed upon them,
and began following
Rabican down the steep
path that led back to their
homelands.

As for Griffen and
Astolpho, they proudly
swooped off to have
adventures all over the
world – even once
flying up to the moon!

HOME
FREE

The Horse and the Colt

By Jean Pierre Claris de Florian

Fables are short stories that illustrate a life lesson or moral, and they often feature animal characters. This horse fable comes from a collection written by a Frenchman in 1792.

THERE WAS ONCE a horse who didn't know what it was like to be owned by humans because he had always lived in the wild. He lived with his son in a pretty meadow, where the streams, the flowers and

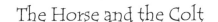

the inviting shade offered everything they needed for their happiness.

His son, a colt, made the most of all these luxuries, stuffing himself every day with clover, fooling away the time on the flowery plain and galloping about without a care in the world. He bathed when he didn't need to and rested even when he wasn't tired.

Time passed and the colt grew fat and lazy. He became bored of having everything he wanted and began to grow dissatisfied. He went to his father and said, sulkily, "Father, for some time I have not been feeling well at all – and I think it's because our surroundings don't suit me any more. This grass is unhealthy and gives me stomach ache, this clover is without smell,

this water is muddy, even the air we breathe here gives me a bad chest. In fact, I really think that unless we go elsewhere, I might get so ill that I may actually die."

The horse, his father, listened carefully and replied, "My dear son, that does sound truly dreadful. We must leave at once."

And as soon as he finished speaking he immediately led the colt off in search of a new home.

The young traveller neighed for joy, but the old one was less merry. He made his child clamber up a steep, dry mountain where there was no grass to eat nor a drop of water to drink. That night, the two were forced to go to bed without supper.

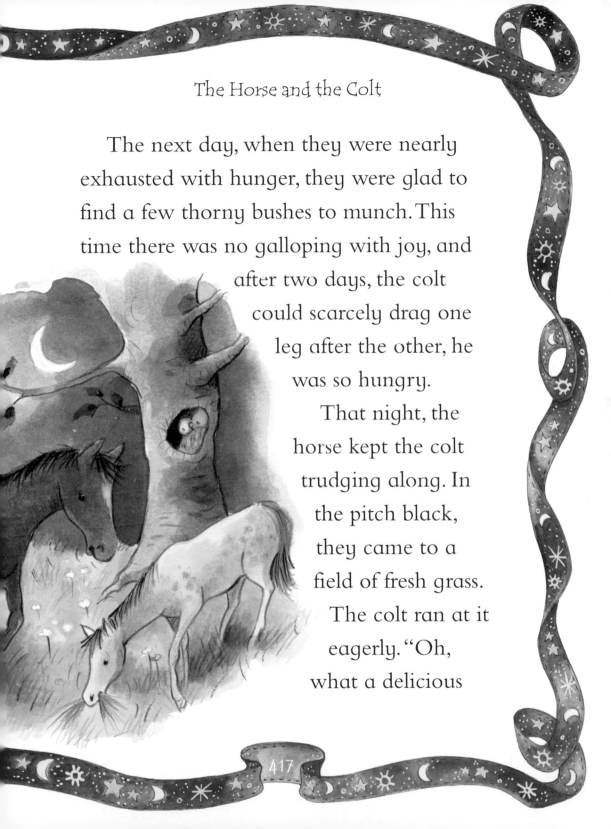

The Horse and the Colt

The next day, when they were nearly exhausted with hunger, they were glad to find a few thorny bushes to munch. This time there was no galloping with joy, and after two days, the colt could scarcely drag one leg after the other, he was so hungry.

That night, the horse kept the colt trudging along. In the pitch black, they came to a field of fresh grass. The colt ran at it eagerly. "Oh, what a delicious banquet!" he exclaimed. "Was there ever anything so sweet and tender?

My father, we will seek no further, let us not return to our old home – let's live forever in this lovely spot!"

As he spoke, the day began to break and the colt recognized his surroundings – he was back in their old meadow! Realizing the lesson his father had taught him, he cast down his eyes in shame. But his father merely said, "My child, in future remember this lesson – he who enjoys too much can become fed up of pleasure. To be happy, one must have not too much and not too little."

The Horse and the Olive

An ancient Greek myth retold
by James Baldwin

ON A STEEP, STONY HILL in ancient
Greece there once lived some very
poor people who had not yet learned to
build houses. They made their homes in
little caves, which they dug in the earth or
hollowed out among the rocks. Their food

was the flesh of wild animals, which they hunted in the woods, with now and then a few berries or nuts. They did not even know how to make bows and arrows, but used slings and clubs and sharp sticks for weapons, and the little clothing they had was made of skins.

They lived on the top of the hill, because they were safe there from savage beasts and the wild men who roamed through the land. The hill was so steep on every side that there was no way of climbing it – save by a single narrow footpath, which was always guarded by someone at the top.

One day when the men were hunting in the woods, they found a strange youth whose face was so fair and who was dressed

so beautifully that they could hardly believe him to be a man like themselves. His body was so slender and he moved so nimbly among the trees, that they fancied him to be a serpent disguised as a human being, and they stood still in wonder. The young man spoke to them, but they could not understand a word that he said.

Then he made signs to them that he was hungry, so they gave him something to eat and were no longer afraid. They wanted their women and children to see the serpent-man, as they called him, and hear him talk, and so they took him home with them to the top of the hill.

They gave the young man some more food and treated him kindly, and he sang

songs to them and talked with their children, and made them happier than they had been for many a day. In a short time he learned to talk in their language, and he told them that his name was Cecrops, and that he had been shipwrecked on the coast not far away, and then he told them many strange things about the land from which he had come and to which he would never be able to return.

The poor people listened and wondered, and it was not long until they began to love him and to look up to him as one wiser than themselves. So Cecrops the serpent-man became the king of the poor people on the hill. He taught them how to make bows and arrows, how to set nets for birds, and how to catch fish with hooks. He led them against the savage wild men of the woods and helped them kill the fierce beasts there. He showed them how to build wooden houses and to thatch them with reeds. And he taught them about the great god Jupiter and the Mighty Folk who lived amid the clouds on the mountain top.

By and by, instead of the wretched caves among the rocks, there was a little town on the top of the hill, with a strong wall and a single narrow gate just where the footpath began to descend to the plain. But as yet the place had no name.

One morning, two strangers were seen in the street. Nobody could tell how they came there. The guard at the gate had not

HOME FREE

seen them, and no man had ever dared to climb the narrow footway without his leave. But there the two strangers stood.

One was a man, the other a woman, and they were so tall, and their faces were so grand and noble, that those who saw them stood still and wondered silently.

The man wore a robe of purple and green and he bore in one hand a strong staff with three sharp spear points at one end.

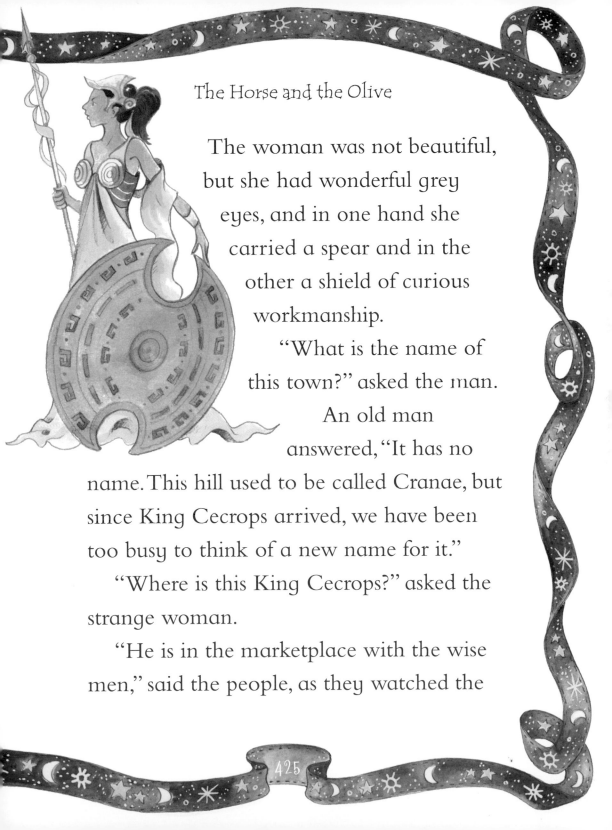

The Horse and the Olive

The woman was not beautiful, but she had wonderful grey eyes, and in one hand she carried a spear and in the other a shield of curious workmanship.

"What is the name of this town?" asked the man.

An old man answered, "It has no name. This hill used to be called Cranae, but since King Cecrops arrived, we have been too busy to think of a new name for it."

"Where is this King Cecrops?" asked the strange woman.

"He is in the marketplace with the wise men," said the people, as they watched the two visitors in wonder.

"Lead us to him at once," said the man.

When Cecrops saw the two strangers coming into the marketplace, he stood up to listen. The man spoke first.

"I am Neptune," said he. "I rule the sea."

"I am Athena," said the woman, "and I give wisdom to people."

"I have come to help you make your town a great city," said Neptune. "Give my name to the place, and let me be your protector and patron, and the wealth of the whole world shall be yours. Ships from every land shall bring you gold and silver, and you shall be the masters of the sea."

"My uncle makes you fair promises," said Athena, "but listen to me. Give my name to

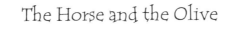

your city, and let me be your patron, and I
will give you that which gold cannot buy –
I will teach you how to do a thousand
things of which you now know nothing. I
will make your city my favourite home, and
I will give you wisdom that shall sway the
minds and hearts of all people until the end
of time."

The king bowed and turned to the
people, who had all crowded into the
marketplace. "Which of these mighty ones
shall we elect to be the protector and patron
of our city?" he asked.

"Neptune and wealth!" cried many.

"Athena and wisdom!" cried the others.

At last when it was plain that the people
could not agree, an old man stood up and

said, "These mighty ones have only given us promises — and who knows which is best? Now, if they would only give us some real gift, right now and right here, which we can see, we would know better how to choose."

"That is true!" cried the people.

"Very well, then," said the strangers, "we will each give you a gift, right now, and then you may choose between us."

Neptune gave the first gift. He stood on the highest point of a hill, raised his three-pointed spear high in the air, and then brought it down with great force on a rock. In a flash, a yawning crevice appeared, out of which there sprang a wonderful creature, white as milk, with long slender legs, an arching neck, and a mane and tail of silk.

HOME FREE

The people had never seen anything like
it before, and they thought it a new kind of
bear or wolf or wild boar. Some of them
ran and hid in their houses, while others
grasped their weapons in alarm. But when
they saw the creature stand quietly by the
side of Neptune, they lost their fear and
came closer to admire its beauty.

"This is my gift," said Neptune. "This
animal will carry your burdens for you, he
will draw your chariots, he will pull your
wagons and your ploughs, he will let you sit
on his back and will run with you faster
than the wind."

"What is his name?" asked the king.

"His name is Horse," answered Neptune.
Then Athena came forwards. She stood

for a moment on a green grassy plot where the children of the town liked to play in the evening. Then she drove the point of her spear deep down into the soil.

At once the air was filled with music, and out of the earth sprang a tree with slender branches, dark green leaves, white flowers and violet-green fruit.

"This is my gift to you," said Athena to the townspeople. "This olive tree will give you food when you are hungry, it will shelter you from the sun when you are faint, it will beautify your city, and the oil from its fruit will be sought by people from all over the world."

"What is it called?" asked the king.

"It is called Olive," answered Athena.

Then the king and his wise men began to talk about the two gifts.

"I do not see that the horse will be of much use to us," said an old man. "As for chariots and wagons and ploughs, we have none of them, and indeed we do not even know what they are. Who among us will ever want to sit on this creature's back and be borne faster than the wind? But the olive tree will be a thing of beauty and a joy for us and our children for years to come."

"Which shall we choose?" asked the king, turning to the people.

"Athena has given us the best gift," they all cried, "and we choose Athena and wisdom!"

"Be it so," said the king, "and the name

of our city shall be Athens."

From that day the town grew and spread, and soon there was not enough room on the hilltop for all the people. When this happened, houses were built in the plain around the foot of the hill, and a great, long road was built to the sea, three miles away. In all the world there was no city more fair than Athens.

In the old marketplace on the top of the hill the people built a temple to Athena, the ruins of which may still be seen. The wonderful olive tree grew and grew and its fruits nourished the town. Many other olive trees sprang from it across Greece, and in all the other countries around the great sea.

As for the horse, he wandered far away

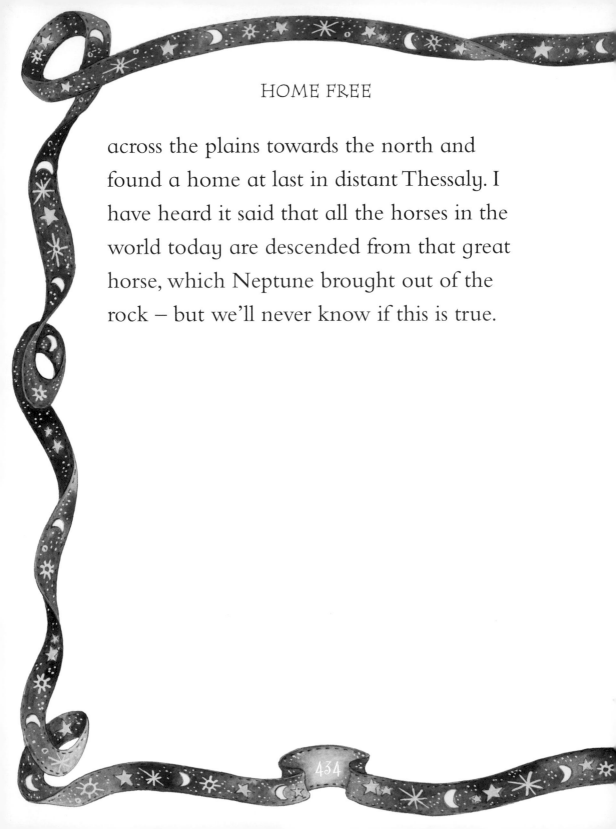

across the plains towards the north and found a home at last in distant Thessaly. I have heard it said that all the horses in the world today are descended from that great horse, which Neptune brought out of the rock – but we'll never know if this is true.

Winding-up Time

From *Mopsa the Fairy* by Jean Ingelow

In this story, a boy called Jack finds a nest of fairies in a
hollow thorn tree. By magic, he journeys on the back of an
albatross, a huge seabird, and then by boat to Fairyland…

JACK LOOKED at the hot brown rocks on
the riverbank until he was quite tired,
but at last the shore became flat. He saw a
beautiful little bay where the water was
still, and where the grass grew down to the
water's edge.

He was so pleased that he cried out hastily, "Oh, how I wish my boat would go into that bay and let me land!"

Jack had no sooner spoke than the boat altered its course, as if somebody had been steering her, and began to make for the bay as fast as she could go.

'How very odd!' thought Jack.

As they drew closer to the bay the water became so shallow that you could see crabs and lobsters walking about on the bottom. At last the boat's keel grated on the pebbles.

Just as Jack began to think of jumping onto the shore, he saw two little old women approaching. They were gently driving a white horse before them. The horse had baskets on each of its sides, and the women

looked like
washer-women.

Jack jumped out of the boat and said to
one of the old women, "Please can you tell
me if this is Fairyland?"

"What did he say?" asked one old
woman of the other.

"He said, 'Is this Fairyland?'" replied the other, who began to empty the baskets of small shirts, coats and stockings. When the women had made them into two little heaps they knelt down and began to wash them in the river, taking no further notice of Jack whatsoever.

Jack stared at them. They were not much taller than himself and they were not taking the slightest care of their clothes. Then he looked at the white horse, who was hanging his head over the lovely, clear water with a very discontented air.

At last the first washer-woman said, "I shall leave off now – I've got a pain."

"Do," said the other. "We'll go home and have a cup of tea."

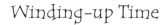

The washer-women wrung out the clothes, put them into the baskets again and, taking the old horse by the bridle, began gently to lead him away.

Jack sprang ashore and said to the boat, "Stay just where you are, will you?" and he ran after the old women, calling to them, "Is there any law to prevent my coming into your country?"

"Woah!" cried the first old woman and the horse stopped, while the second woman repeated, "Any law? No, not that I know of – but if you are a stranger here you had better look out."

"Why?" asked Jack.

"You don't suppose, do you," one of the washer-women said to the other, "that our

queen will wind up strangers?"

While Jack was wondering what she meant, the other said, "I shouldn't wonder if he lasts eight days. Gee!" and the horse went on.

"No, woah!" said the other woman.

"No, no. Gee! I tell you," cried the first.

Upon this, to Jack's astonishment, the old horse stopped, and said, "Now, then, which is it to be? I'm willing to gee, and I'm agreeable to woah, but what's a horse to do when you say both together?"

"Why, he talks!" said Jack.

"Yes, it's because he's got a head cold," observed one of the washer-women. "He always talks when he's got a cold, and there's no pleasing him. Whatever you say, he's just not satisfied. Gee, Boney, do!"

"Gee it is, then," said the horse, and it began to jog on.

"He spoke again!" said Jack and the horse laughed. Jack was quite alarmed.

"It appears that horses from your land don't talk?" observed the first woman.

"Never," answered Jack, "they can't."

"You mean they won't," observed the horse. And though he spoke the words of mankind, it was in a different voice. Jack felt that the horse's voice was just the natural tone for a horse and that it did not arise

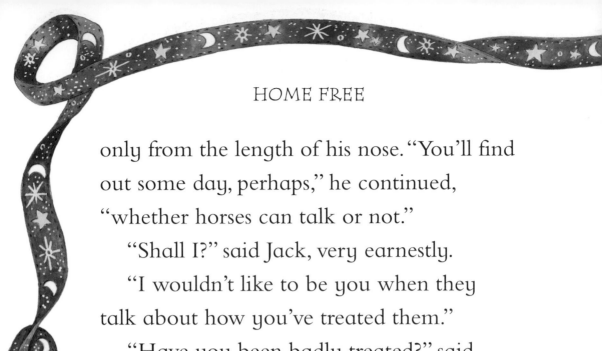

only from the length of his nose. "You'll find out some day, perhaps," he continued, "whether horses can talk or not."

"Shall I?" said Jack, very earnestly.

"I wouldn't like to be you when they talk about how you've treated them."

"Have you been badly treated?" said Jack to the horse, in an anxious tone.

"Yes, yes, of course he has," one of the women broke in, "but he has come here to get all right again. This is a very wholesome country for horses, isn't it, Boney?"

"Yes," said the horse.

"Well, then, jog on, there's a dear," continued the old woman. "Why, you will be young again soon, you know – young, playful, merry and handsome. You'll be

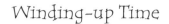

quite a colt, by and by, and then we shall
set you free to join your companions in the
happy meadows."

The old horse was so comforted by this
kind speech that he pricked up his ears and
quickened his pace considerably.

"Pray, are you a boy?" asked the second
old woman.

"Yes," said Jack, as he skipped along to
keep up.

"A real boy, that doesn't need winding
up?" inquired the old woman.

"I don't know what you mean,"
answered Jack, "but I am a real boy,
certainly."

"Ah!" she replied. "I thought you were,
by the way Boney spoke to you. Real

people worked Boney hard, and often drove him about all night in the miserable streets, and never let him have so much as a canter in a green field," said one of the women, "but he'll be all right now, only he has to begin at the wrong end."

"What do you mean?" said Jack.

"Why, in this country," answered the old woman, "the horses begin by being terribly old and stiff, and they seem miserable at first, but slowly they get young again, as you heard me reminding him."

"Indeed," said Jack, "and do you like it that way?"

"It has nothing to do with me," she answered. "We are here to take care of all the creatures men have ill used. They are

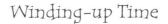

very sick and old when first they come to us. But then we take care of them and gradually bring them up to be young and happy once more."

"This must be a very nice country to live in, then," said Jack.

"For horses it is," said the old lady, significantly.

"Well," said Jack, "it does seem very full of haystacks, certainly, and all the air smells just like fresh grass."

At this moment they came to a beautiful, wildflower meadow, and the old horse stopped, and, turning to the first woman, said, "Faxa, I think I could fancy a handful of clover."

Upon this, Faxa snatched Jack's cap off

his head, jumped over a little ditch, and gathering some clover, presently brought it back full, handing it to the old horse with great civility.

"You shouldn't be in such a hurry," observed the old horse, "you'll wind down if you don't take care."

Just then, a little man dressed like a groom came running up, out of breath. "Come along! I hear the bell, and we are a good way from the palace!"

Jack heard a bell ringing violently from some distance away, and when the groom began to run, he ran beside him. Jack

thought he should like to
see the palace, and
understand the
strange things the
washer-women had
spoken about.

As they ran, people
gathered from all sides –
fields, cottages, mills –
till at last there was
quite a crowd, among
whom Jack saw the two washer-women.
They were all heading for a large house, the
wide door of which was open.

Jack stood with the crowd, and peeped
in. There was a woman sitting inside upon a
rocking-chair – a tall, large woman,

wearing a gold-coloured gown – and beside her stood a table, covered with things that looked like keys.

"What is that woman doing?" Jack asked Faxa, who was standing close to him.

"Winding us up, to be sure," answered Faxa. "You don't suppose, surely, that we can go on for ever?"

"Extraordinary!" said Jack. "Are you wound up every evening, like watches?"

"Unless we have misbehaved ourselves," she answered, "and then she lets us run right the way down."

"And what then?"

"What then?" repeated Faxa, "why, then we have to stop and stand against a wall, till she is pleased to forgive us, and let our

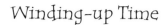

friends carry us in to be wound up again."

Jack looked in. He saw the people enter and stand close by the woman. One after the other she took them by the chin with her left hand and with her right hand found a key that pleased her. It seemed to Jack that there was a tiny keyhole in the back of their heads, and that she put the key in to wind them up.

"You must take your turn with the others," said the groom.

"There's no keyhole in my head," said Jack, "besides, I do not want anyone to wind me up."

"But you must do as others do," he persisted, "and if you have no keyhole, our queen can easily have one made."

"Make one in my head!" exclaimed Jack. "She shall do no such thing!"

"We shall see," said Faxa, quietly. And Jack was so frightened that he set off and ran back towards the river as fast as his legs would carry him.

Many of the people called to him to stop, but they could not run after him, because they wanted winding up. However, they would certainly have caught him if he had not been very quick, for before he got to the river he heard behind him the footsteps of the queen's attendants. He sprang into the boat just before they reached the edge of the water.

As soon as he jumped aboard, the boat swung round and moved out into the

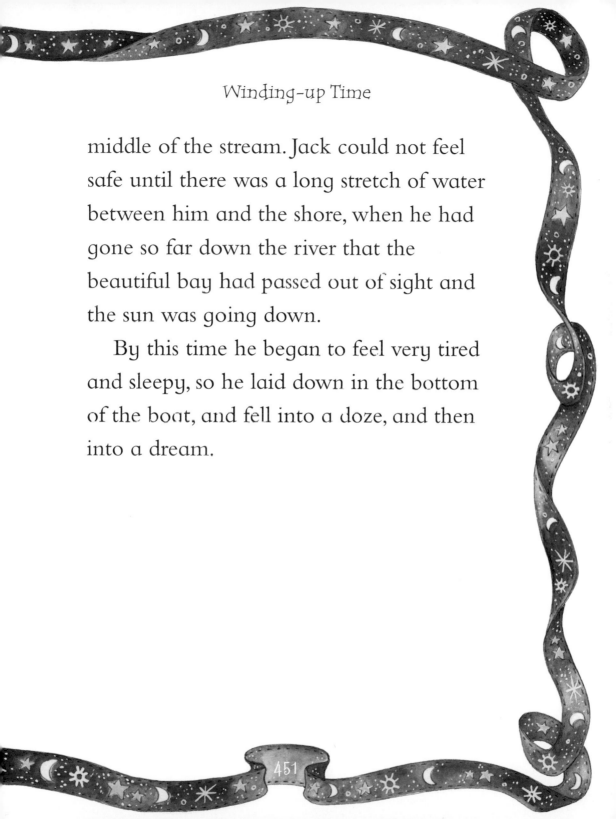

middle of the stream. Jack could not feel safe until there was a long stretch of water between him and the shore, when he had gone so far down the river that the beautiful bay had passed out of sight and the sun was going down.

By this time he began to feel very tired and sleepy, so he laid down in the bottom of the boat, and fell into a doze, and then into a dream.

Jupiter
and the
Horse

By Gotthold Ephraim Lessing

This story is taken from a collection of fables written by a German man in 1759. It features a horse and the chief god in Roman mythology, Jupiter.

ONE DAY, the horse boldly approached the throne of Jupiter and said, "Father of all humans and creatures, everyone agrees that I am one of the most beautiful animals that you created to bless the world

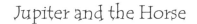

– and I'm inclined to agree. But I've given it quite a bit of thought, and I reckon that there are still many ways in which I could be improved."

"And what do you think could be improved?" said Jupiter, with a wry, knowing smile. "Speak, I am all ready to receive your instructions."

"Great," said the horse boldly, "then I could perhaps be even faster, with longer, more slender legs. Oh, and I wouldn't mind having an arched neck, like that of the graceful swan. A broader chest would increase my strength. And lastly, as you have created me to carry humans – your favourite creature of all – you might consider giving me a ready-made saddle, so people don't have to use their own."

"Well then," said Jupiter, "wait just a moment." His face became very thoughtful and serious and, holding up his hands, he spoke the magic words of creation.

A cloud of dust blew up from the ground. It whirled into a huge shape, grew solid and then began to move. And suddenly in front of his throne there stood – the awkward and clumsy camel!

The horse stared at the new creature from its head to its toes and gave a shudder of disgust.

"So, here are the longer, slimmer legs," explained Jupiter. "And look, it has an arched neck, a broader chest and a useful saddle. So shall I make you look like this?"

Jupiter and the Horse

The horse, all aquiver with fear, dared not say anything to Jupiter, and stayed very quiet indeed.

"I should think so too," said Jupiter firmly. "Go on your way then – I won't punish you as long as you have learned your lesson. But I shall leave this new creature just as he is, to remind you of how

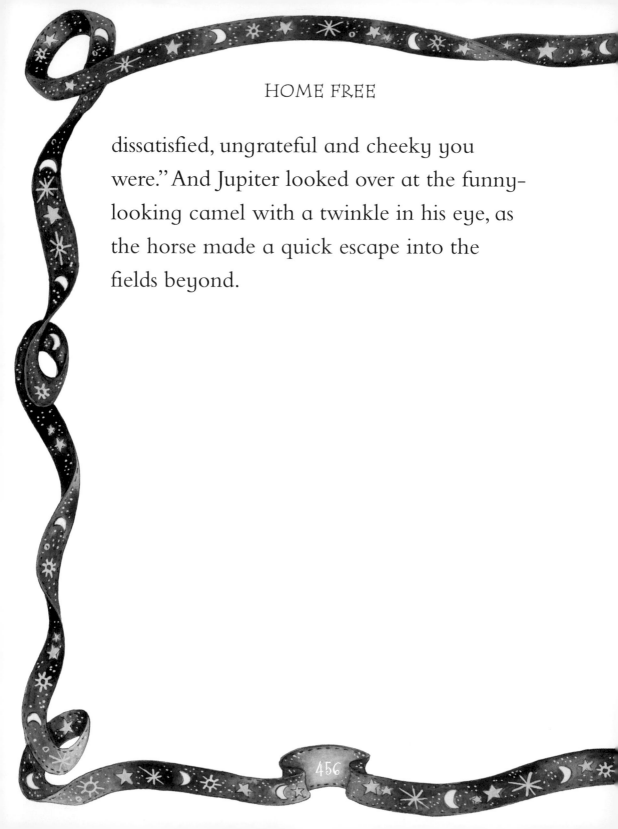

dissatisfied, ungrateful and cheeky you were." And Jupiter looked over at the funny-looking camel with a twinkle in his eye, as the horse made a quick escape into the fields beyond.

The Hippogriff

From *The Book of Beasts* by E Nesbit

A hippogriff is a creature that appears in myths from several different countries. It was supposed to be the offspring of a mare and a griffin - another legendary creature that had the body of a lion and the head and wings of an eagle.

LIONEL WENT DOWN INTO the library. The prime minister and the chancellor were there, and when they saw the new boy king they bowed very low, and were about to ask Lionel most politely what he was coming for when Lionel cried out, "Oh, what a worldful of books! Are they yours?"

"They are yours, Your Majesty," answered the chancellor. "They were the property of the late king, your great-great—"

"Yes, I know," Lionel interrupted. "Well, I shall read them all. I love to read. I am so glad I learned to read."

"If I might venture to advise Your Majesty," said the prime minister, "I should not read these books. Your great-great-great…"

"Yes?" said Lionel, quickly.

"He was a very good king, oh yes, really a superior king in his way, but he was a little – well, strange."

"Why?" said Lionel, puzzled.

"Well, the fact is," the chancellor explained, twisting his red beard in an agitated way, "your great…"

"Go on," said Lionel.

"…was called a wizard. And I wouldn't advise touching his books."

"Just this one," cried Lionel, laying his hands on the cover of a brown book that lay on the study table. It had gold patterns on the leather and gold clasps with turquoises and rubies in the twists of them, and gold corners.

"I must look at this one," Lionel said, for on the back in big letters he read – *The Book of Beasts*.

The chancellor sighed and said, "Don't be a silly little king."

But Lionel had already got the gold clasps undone. He opened the first page and there was a butterfly so beautifully painted that it looked as if it were alive.

"There," said Lionel, "isn't the butterfly just lovely?"

But as he spoke the butterfly fluttered its many-coloured wings on the old page of the book, and flew up and out of the open window.

"Well!" said the prime minister. "That's magic, that is."

But the king had already turned the next page. There was a beautiful

blue bird, under which
was written, 'Blue Bird
of Paradise', and while
the king gazed enchanted
at the charming picture the
blue bird fluttered his wings on
the page, then spread them
wide and flew out of the book.
Then the prime
minister snatched the
book away from
Lionel and shut it
upon the blank page
where the bird had been, and put it on a
very high shelf, out of Lionel's reach.

The chancellor gave the king a good
telling off, and said, "You're a naughty,

Butterfly

disobedient little king!" He was very angry.

"I don't see that I've done any harm," said Lionel.

"No harm?" said the chancellor. "Ah, but what might have been on the next page? A snake, or something like that."

"Well, I'm sorry if I've made you cross," said Lionel. "Come, let's be friends."

So he made up with the prime minister, and they settled down for a nice quiet game of noughts and crosses while the chancellor went to add up his money.

But when Lionel was in bed he could not sleep for thinking of the book, and when the full moon was shining he got up and crept down to the library, climbed up and got *The Book of Beasts*.

The Hippogriff

He took it outside to the terrace, where the moonlight was as bright as day, and he opened the book. He saw the empty pages with 'Butterfly' and 'Blue Bird of Paradise' underneath, and then he turned onto the next page.

There was some sort of red thing sitting under a palm tree, and under it was written 'Dragon'. The dragon did not move, and the king shut up the book rather quickly and went back to bed.

But the next day he wanted another look, so he took the book out into the garden, and when he undid the clasps with the rubies and turquoises, the book opened all by itself at the picture with dragon underneath, and the sun shone on the page.

HOME FREE

And then, quite suddenly, a great red dragon came out of the book! It spread its vast, scarlet wings and flew away across the garden to the far hills. Lionel was left with the empty page before him.

The Hippogriff

And then Lionel felt that he had indeed gone and done it. He had not yet been king twenty-four hours, and already he had let loose a red dragon on his citizens.

Lionel began to cry. The chancellor and the prime minister and the nurse all came running to see what was the matter. And when they saw the book they understood. The prime minister and the chancellor hurried off to consult the police and see what could be done.

Everyone did what they could. They sat on committees and stood on guard, and lay in wait for the dragon, but it stayed up in the hills, and there was nothing more to be done. The faithful nurse, meanwhile, put the king to bed without any supper.

HOME FREE

Now, the next day was Saturday. And in the afternoon the dragon suddenly swooped down upon the common in all his hideous redness, and carried off the football players, umpires, goalposts, ball and all.

The dragon stayed asleep till the following Saturday, but then it woke up with a terrible hunger and ate the prime minister and all the members of parliament.

And when the next Saturday came around, it ate an entire orphanage, before going to rest under a tree. The dragon had to go to rest under a tree or it would have caught fire from the heat of the sun. You see, the dragon was very hot to begin with and it couldn't take much more heat.

The Saturday after that, the dragon

actually walked into the royal nursery and carried off the king's own pet rocking horse.

At last Lionel had an idea. He carried *The Book of Beasts* out into the rose garden, and opened it – very quickly, so that he might not be afraid and change his mind. The book fell open wide, almost in the middle, and written at the bottom of the page was the word 'Hippogriff'.

And before Lionel had time to see what the picture was, there was a fluttering of great wings and a stamping of hoofs, and a sweet, soft, friendly neighing – and out of the book came a beautiful white horse with a long white mane and a long white tail.

The horse had great wings like a swan, and the softest, kindest eyes in the world. It stood there among the roses, and rubbed its silky-soft, milky white nose against the little king's shoulder, and the little king thought,

'But for your wings you are very like my dear lost rocking horse.' Nearby, a blue bird was singing very loudly and sweetly.

Suddenly, the king saw the great straggling, sprawling, wicked shape of the red dragon in the sky. He knew at once what he must do. He caught up *The Book of Beasts*, jumped on the back of the gentle, beautiful hippogriff, and leaning down he whispered in its white ear: "Fly, dear hippogriff, fly your very fastest to the Pebbly Waste."

And when the dragon saw them start, it turned and flew after them, with his great wings flapping like clouds at sunset.

The Hippogriff's wide wings were snowy as clouds at moonrise. And the white-winged horse flew farther and farther away, with the dragon pursuing, till he reached the very middle of the Pebbly Waste.

Now, the Pebbly Waste is just like the parts of the seaside where there is no sand – all round, loose, shifting stones, and there is no grass there and no tree within a hundred miles of it.

Lionel jumped off the white horse's back in the very middle of the Pebbly Waste, and hurriedly unclasped *The Book of Beasts*. He laid it open on the pebbles and had just jumped back onto his white horse when up came the dragon.

It was flying very feebly and looking around everywhere for a tree, for it was just on the stroke of twelve midday, the sun was

shining like a gold coin in the blue sky, and there was not a tree for a hundred miles.

The white-winged horse sprang into the air and flew around and around the dragon as it writhed on the dry pebbles. It was getting very hot – indeed, parts of the dragon had even begun to smoke. It knew that it would certainly catch fire in another minute unless it could get under a tree.

The dragon made a snatch with his red claws at the king and the hippogriff, but was too feeble to reach them, and besides, it did not dare to overexert itself for fear it should get even hotter.

It was then that the dragon saw *The Book of Beasts* lying on the pebbles, open at the page with 'Dragon' written at the bottom. It looked and hesitated, and looked again, and then, with one last squirm of rage, wriggled itself back into the picture, and sat down under the palm tree. The page was a little singed as he went in.

As soon as Lionel saw that the dragon had been obliged to go and sit under its own palm tree, he jumped off his horse and shut the book with a bang.

"Oh, hurrah!" he cried. "Now we really have done it."

And he clasped the book very tightly.

"Oh, my precious hippogriff," he cried. "You are the bravest, dearest, most beautiful—"

"Hush," whispered the hippogriff modestly. "We are not alone."

The Hippogriff

And indeed there was quite a crowd around them on the Pebbly Waste. The prime minister, the members of parliament, the football players, the children from the orphanage, the rocking horse, and indeed everyone who had been eaten by the dragon, were there. You see, it was impossible for the dragon to take them into the book, so it had to leave them outside.

And so they all went home and lived happy ever after – the hippogriff content in the greenest of green pastures.

A Horse Fair

From *Black Beauty* by Anna Sewell

As a colt, Black Beauty enjoyed a carefree life on a farm. Then
he worked for a kind country squire, pulling his carriages. However,
he is later bought by owners who treat him badly. After damaging
his knees in an accident, he is sent to be sold at a horse fair.

NO DOUBT A HORSE FAIR is a very
amusing place to those who have
nothing to lose – at any rate, there is plenty
to see. Long strings of young horses out of
the country, fresh from the marshes, droves

of shaggy little Welsh ponies, and hundreds
of cart horses, some of them with their long
tails braided up and tied with scarlet cord.
There are a good many like myself,
handsome and high-bred, but fallen into
the middle class, through some accident or
overwork or old age.

There were some splendid animals quite
in their prime, and fit for anything. They
were throwing out their legs and showing
off their paces in high style, as they were
trotted out with a leading rein, the groom
running by the side.

But round in the background there were
a number of poor things, sadly broken down
with hard work, with their knees knuckling
over and their hind legs swinging out at

every step, and there were some very dejected-looking old horses, with the under lip hanging down and the ears lying back heavily, as if there were no more pleasure in life, and no more hope. There were some so thin you might see all their ribs, and some with old sores on their backs and hips.

These were sad sights for a horse to look upon, because one knows that one might end up in the same state.

There was a great deal of bargaining, of running up and beating down, and if a horse may speak his mind so far as he understands, I should say there were more lies told and more trickery at that horse fair than a clever man could ever give an account of.

A Horse Fair

I was put with two or three other strong, useful-looking horses, and a good many people came to look at us.

The first thing was to pull my mouth open, then to look at my eyes, then feel all the way down my legs, and give me a hard feel of the skin and flesh, and then try my paces. The difference there was in the way these things were done was wonderful.

Some did it in a rough, offhand way, as if one was only a piece of wood, while others would take their hands gently over one's body, with a pat now and then, as much as to say, "By your leave." Of course I judged a good deal of the buyers by their manners to myself.

There was one man, I thought, if he

would buy me, I should be happy. He was
not a gentleman, nor yet one of the loud,
flashy sort that call themselves so. He was
rather a small man, but well made, and
quite nimble. I knew in a moment by the
way he handled me, that he was used to
caring for horses.

He spoke gently, and his grey eye
had a kindly, cheery look in it. It may
seem strange to say, but the clean,
fresh smell there
was about him
made me take to
him – a fresh smell

as if he had just come out of a hayloft.

He offered twenty-three pounds for me, but that was refused, and he walked away. I looked after him, but he was gone, and a very hard-looking, loud-voiced man came. I was dreadfully afraid he would have me, but he walked off. One or two more came who did not mean business.

Then the hard-faced man came back again and offered twenty-three pounds. A very close bargain was being driven, for my salesman began to think he should not get all he asked, and must come down in price… but just then the grey-eyed man came back again. I could not help reaching out my head towards him. He stroked my face kindly.

"Well, old chap," he said, "I think we should suit each other. I'll give twenty-four for him."

"Say twenty-five and you shall have a deal my friend."

"Twenty-four ten," said my friend, in a very decided tone, "and not another sixpence – yes or no?"

"Done," said the salesman, "and you may depend upon it there's a great deal of quality in that horse – he's a bargain."

The money was paid on the spot, and my new master took my halter, and led me out of the fair to an inn, where he had a saddle and bridle ready.

He gave me a good feed of oats, which I very was grateful for, and he stood by while I ate it, talking to himself and talking to me.

Half an hour after we were on our way to London, through pleasant lanes and country roads, until we came into the great London thoroughfare, on which we travelled steadily, till in the twilight we reached the great city.

The gas lamps were already lighted. There were streets to the right, and streets to the left, and streets crossing each other, for mile upon mile. I thought we should never come to the end of them. At last, in passing through one, we came to a long cab stand, when my rider called out in a cheery voice, "Goodnight, governor!"

"Hello!" cried a voice. "Have you got a good one?"

"I think so," replied my owner.

"I wish you luck with him."

"Thank you, governor," and he rode on. We soon turned up one of the side streets, and about halfway up that we turned into a very narrow street, with rather poor-looking houses on one side, and what seemed to be coach-houses and stables on the other.

My owner pulled up at one of the houses

and whistled. Straight away the door flew open, and a young woman, followed by a little girl and boy, ran out to meet us. There was a very lively greeting as my rider dismounted.

"Now, then, Harry, my boy, open the gates, and mother will bring us the lantern."

The next minute they were all standing round me in a small stable-yard.

"Is he gentle, father?"

"Yes, Dolly, as gentle as your own kitten – come and pat him."

At once the little hand was patting about all over my shoulder without fear. How good it felt!

"Let me get him a bran mash while you rub him down," said the mother.

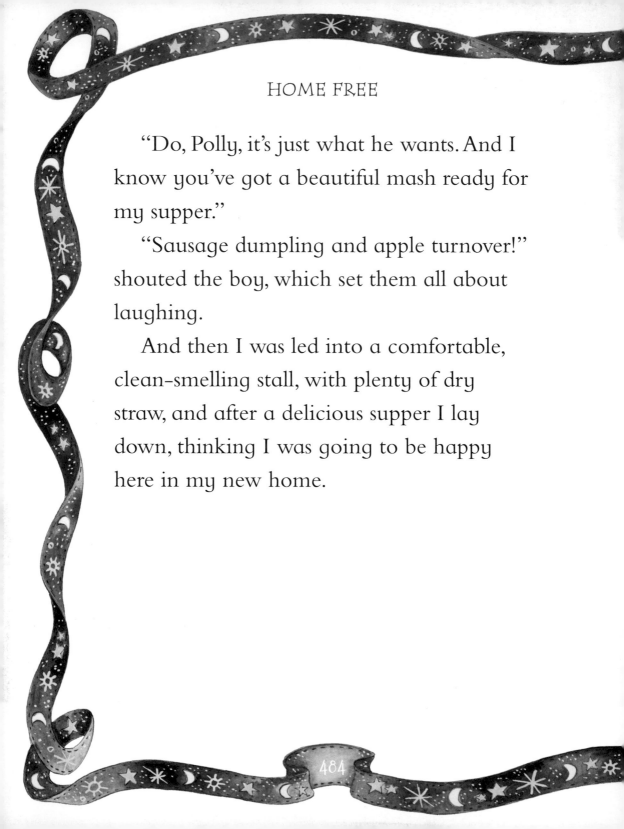

"Do, Polly, it's just what he wants. And I know you've got a beautiful mash ready for my supper."

"Sausage dumpling and apple turnover!" shouted the boy, which set them all about laughing.

And then I was led into a comfortable, clean-smelling stall, with plenty of dry straw, and after a delicious supper I lay down, thinking I was going to be happy here in my new home.

The Seven Foals

A retelling of a traditional Norwegian fairytale by Sir George Webbe Dasent

ONCE UPON A TIME there was a very poor couple who lived in a wretched hut, far away in the wood. They had three sons, and the youngest of them was known as Boots.

One day the eldest lad said he would go

out to seek his fortune. He walked and walked the whole day and, when evening drew in, came to a king's palace. The king was out on the steps. He asked where the lad was going.

"Oh, I'm wandering about, looking for a job," said the lad.

"Will you serve me," asked the king, "and watch my seven foals? If you can watch them one whole day, and tell me at night what they eat and what they drink, you shall marry the princess and have half my kingdom."

The lad thought that would be an easy task, so next morning at dawn, the king's coachman let out the seven foals. Off they dashed over hill and dale, through bush and

bog, and away the lad tore after them.
When he had run a long time, he began to
get weary. He came to a cleft in a rock,
where an old hag sat at a spinning wheel.
"Come hither, my pretty son, and let me
comb your hair," she cried out.

The lad was only too willing to rest, so

he sat down in the cleft of the rock with the old hag, and laid his head on her lap. She combed his hair all day whilst he lay there, and stretched his lazy bones.

In the evening, the old hag said, "The king's foals will soon pass by here again, then you can run back to the palace with them, and no one will know that you have lain here all day long instead of finding out what they eat and drink."

When they came, she gave the lad a flask of water and a clod of turf. He was to show them to the king, and say that was what his seven foals ate and drank. So the lad headed back with the foals to the palace.

But when the king saw the lad looking so cool and refreshed, and was shown the flask of water and clod of turf, he knew that the lad had not watched the foals all day as he had promised.

He was so furious that he ordered his guards to chase him all the way home.

The next day the second son said he would go out into the world to try his luck. He walked all day until he too came to the king's palace. He also took on the challenge for the same reward.

In the grey of the morning, the coachman let out the seven foals, and off they went again over hill and dale, through bush and bog, and the second son went after them. But exactly the same thing happened to him as his brother.

He met the old hag and rested, and

when the foals came back at nightfall, he
too got a flask of water and clod of turf
from the old hag to show to the king. Once
again, the king saw through the lad's
deception and told his guards to chase the
lad all the way home.

On the third day the youngest brother
set out, even though his brothers scoffed at
him and swore he would do no better than
they had.

After he had walked the whole day, he
too came at dusk to the king's palace. There
stood the king out on the steps, and he
asked where the youngest lad was bound.

Boots explained that he was the brother
of the two lads who had watched the king's
seven foals without success. He asked if he

too might try to watch them the next day.

"Oh, stuff!" said the king crossly. "If you're brother to those two, you're not worth much, I'll be bound. But I suppose I should give you a chance."

So the next morning, at the grey of dawn, the coachman let out the seven foals again, and away they went over hill and dale, through bush and bog, and Boots went on behind them.

And so, when he too had run a long while, he came to the cleft in the rock, where the old hag sat, spinning at her distaff. She called out to Boots, "Come hither, my pretty son, and let me comb your hair."

But Boots didn't fall for her trick!

The Seven Foals

"Don't you wish you may catch me!" said Boots, and he kept running along, leaping and jumping, holding onto one of the foal's tails as they cantered.

And when he had got well past the cleft in the rock, the youngest foal said, "Jump up on my back, my lad, for we've a long way to go."

So Boots jumped up on his back and they rode on and on for a very long time.

"Do you see anything now?" said the youngest foal.

"No, nothing," said Boots.

They travelled on farther.

"Do you see anything now?" asked the foal again.

"I don't see a thing," said the lad.

HOME FREE

After they had gone a great, great way
farther, the foal asked again, "Do you see
anything now?"

"Yes," said Boots, "now I see something
that looks white – its just like a tall, big
birch trunk."

"Yes, that's just what it is" said the foal,
"and we're going inside it."

So when they got to the tree, the eldest
foal pushed it on one side, and a door
appeared. Inside the door was a
little room, and in the room
there was scarcely
anything but

a little fireplace and one or two benches.
But behind the door hung a great rusty
sword and a little pitcher.

"Can you brandish the sword?" said the
foals. "Try it now."

Boots tried, but he couldn't lift it. So the
foals told him to drink from the pitcher, first
once, then twice and then three times. After
this he could wield the sword easily.

"Now you may take the sword
with you and carry out an
important task. You see, we used
to all be princes, but an ugly troll
has thrown this shape over us.

The only way for us to return to
our true form is for you to cut off
our heads with the sword on your

wedding day. For we are the brothers of the
princess who you are to marry, once you
can tell the king what we eat and drink.
But remember this – after you have cut off
each of our seven heads, you must place the
right head with the right body. Then the
spell will have no more power over us."

Boots promised to do all of that, and
then on they went back to the palace.
When they had travelled a long, long way,
the foal asked, "Do you see anything?"

"No," said Boots.

So they travelled a good bit further still.

"And now?" asked the foal.

"No, I see nothing," said Boots.

So they travelled many miles again, over
hill and dale, through bush and bog.

"Do you see anything now?" said the foal to Boots.

"Yes," said Boots, "now I see something like a blue stripe, far away."

"Yes," said the foal, "that's a river we've got to cross."

Over the river was a long, grand bridge, and when they had got over to the other side, they travelled on a long, long way. At last the Foal asked again, "Do you see anything now?"

"Yes, this time I see something – it's a church steeple."

"Yes," said the Foal, "that's where we're going to turn in."

When the foals got into the churchyard, they became men. They looked like princes, with fine clothes that glistened.

They went into the church, and took the bread and wine from the priest who stood at the altar. Boots went in too, and watched. When they left, Boots took a flask of wine and a wafer with him.

As soon as the seven princes came out of the church and into the churchyard, they changed back into foals again, and so Boots got up on the back of the youngest, and so they travelled back the same way that they had come – only this time they went much, much faster.

First they crossed the bridge, next they passed the trunk, and then they passed the old hag, who sat at the cleft and span, and they went by her so fast, that Boots couldn't

hear what the old hag screeched after him – but he heard enough to know she was in an awful rage.

It was almost dark when they got back to the palace, and the king himself stood out on the steps and waited for them.

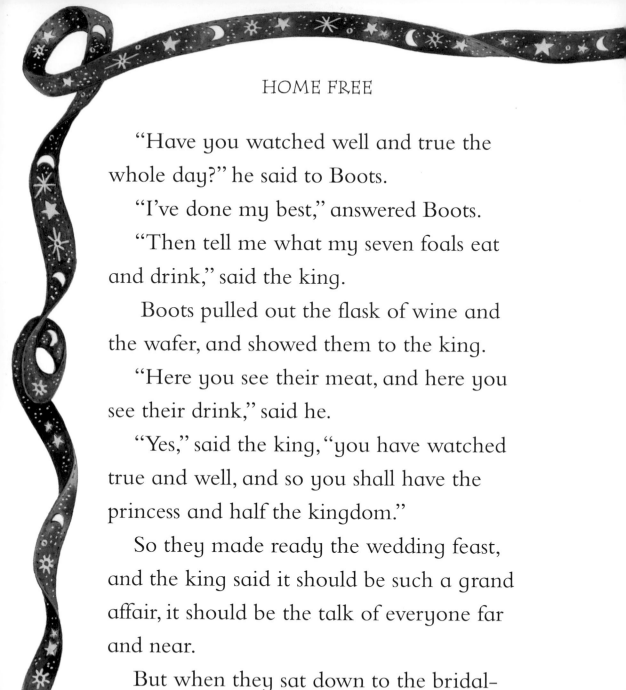

"Have you watched well and true the whole day?" he said to Boots.

"I've done my best," answered Boots.

"Then tell me what my seven foals eat and drink," said the king.

Boots pulled out the flask of wine and the wafer, and showed them to the king.

"Here you see their meat, and here you see their drink," said he.

"Yes," said the king, "you have watched true and well, and so you shall have the princess and half the kingdom."

So they made ready the wedding feast, and the king said it should be such a grand affair, it should be the talk of everyone far and near.

But when they sat down to the bridal-

feast, the bridegroom got up and went down to the stable, for he said he had forgotten something, and must go and fetch it straight away.

And when he got down there, he did as the foals had asked, and he cut their heads off, all seven – the eldest first, and the others after him. He took great care to lay each head at the tail of the foal to which it belonged, and as he did this, they all became princes once more!

So when he returned to the bridal hall with the seven princes, the king was so glad he both kissed Boots and patted him on the back, and his bride was still more glad of him than she had been before.

"Half the kingdom you have got

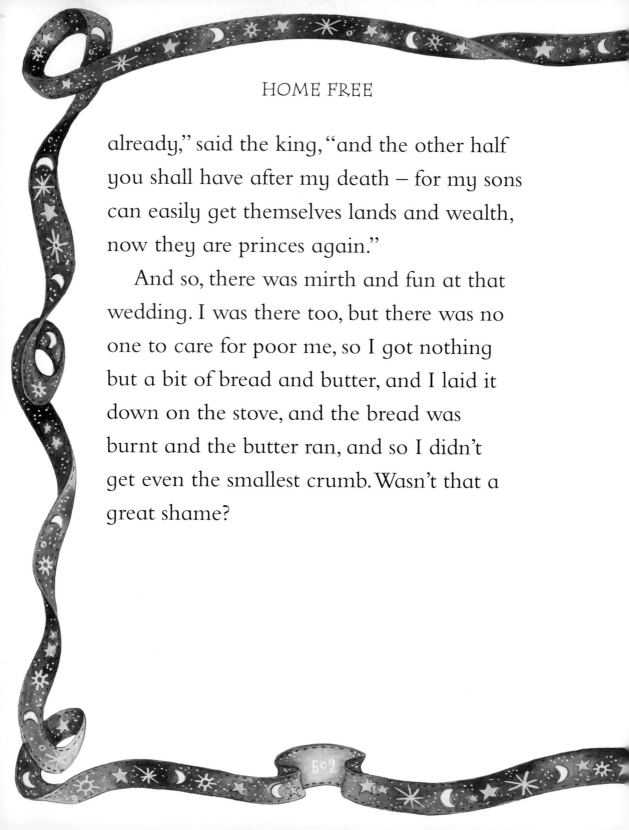

already," said the king, "and the other half
you shall have after my death – for my sons
can easily get themselves lands and wealth,
now they are princes again."

And so, there was mirth and fun at that
wedding. I was there too, but there was no
one to care for poor me, so I got nothing
but a bit of bread and butter, and I laid it
down on the stove, and the bread was
burnt and the butter ran, and so I didn't
get even the smallest crumb. Wasn't that a
great shame?

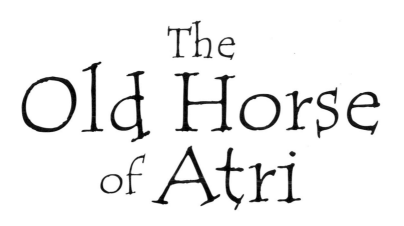

The Old Horse of Atri

A version of a traditional Italian
folktale by James Baldwin

ATRI IS THE NAME of a little town in
Italy. It is a very old town and is built
halfway up the side of a steep hill.

A long time ago, the king of Atri bought
a fine large bell and had it hung up in a

tower in the marketplace. It was a very pretty bell, polished until it looked almost as bright and yellow as the sun, and attached to it was a rope so long that even the smallest child could reach it.

Then the king made an announcement to the townspeople. "This is the bell of justice," he proclaimed. "It is your bell, but it must never be rung unless someone is in need of judgement. If any one of you is wronged, he may come and ring the bell and then the judges shall come together at once, and hear his case, and give him justice. Rich and poor, old and young, all alike may come – but no one must touch the rope unless he knows that he has been wronged."

Many years passed by after this. Many times did the bell in the marketplace ring out to call the judges together. Many wrongs were righted, many ill-doers were punished. At last the rope was almost worn out. The lower part of it was untwisted and the strands were broken. It became so short that only a tall man could reach it.

"This will never do," said the judges one day. "What if a child should be wronged? It could not ring the bell to let us know."

They gave orders that a new rope should
be put upon the bell at once, a rope that
should hang right down to the ground so
that everyone could reach it. But there was
not a rope to be found in all Atri. They
would have to send across the mountains
for one and it would be many days before it
could be brought. What if some great
wrong should be done before it came? How
could the judges know about it, if the
injured one could not reach the old rope?

"Let me fix it for you," said a man who
stood by. He ran into his garden, which was
not far away, and soon came back with a
long grapevine in his hands. He climbed up
and fastened it to the bell and the slender
vine, with its leaves and tendrils still upon it,

trailed to the ground.

"Yes," said the judges, "it is a very good rope. Let it be as it is."

Now, on the hillside above the village, there lived a man who had once been a brave knight and fought many battles. His best friend had been his horse – a strong, noble steed that had borne him safe through many a danger. But the knight, as he had grown old, had come to care for nothing but hoarding gold. At last he sold all that he had, except his horse, and went to live in a little hut on the hillside.

Day after day he sat among his money bags and planned how he might get more gold. Day after day his horse stood in his bare stall, half-starved, and shivering.

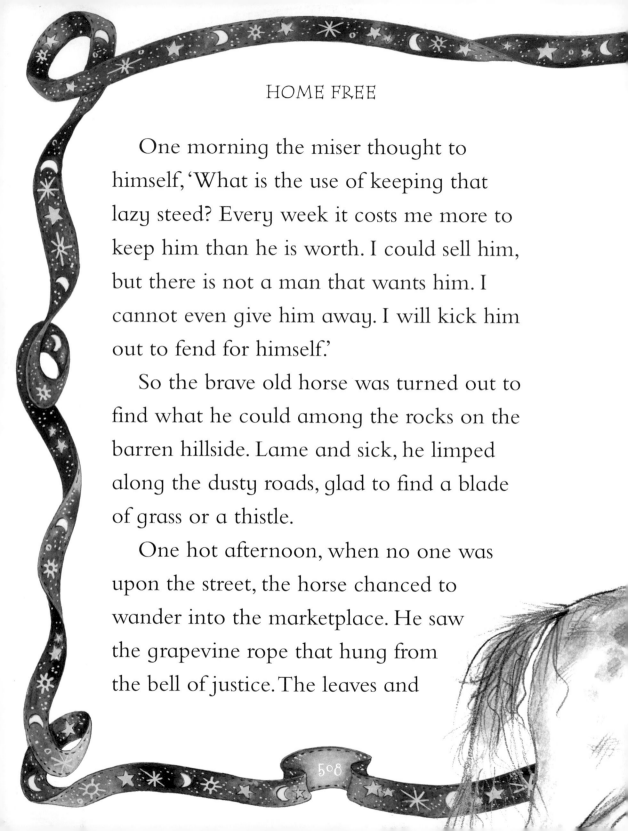

HOME FREE

One morning the miser thought to himself, 'What is the use of keeping that lazy steed? Every week it costs me more to keep him than he is worth. I could sell him, but there is not a man that wants him. I cannot even give him away. I will kick him out to fend for himself.'

So the brave old horse was turned out to find what he could among the rocks on the barren hillside. Lame and sick, he limped along the dusty roads, glad to find a blade of grass or a thistle.

One hot afternoon, when no one was upon the street, the horse chanced to wander into the marketplace. He saw the grapevine rope that hung from the bell of justice. The leaves and

The Old Horse of Atri

tendrils upon it were still fresh and green,
for it had not been there long. What a fine
dinner for a starving horse! He stretched his
thin neck, and took one of the tempting
morsels in his mouth. He pulled at it and
the great bell above him began to ring.

The judges heard it and put on their
robes and went out
through the hot streets
to the marketplace.
They wondered
who it could
be who

would ring the bell at such a time.

"Ha!" cried one, when he saw the old horse nibbling at the vine. "It is the miser's steed. He has come to call for justice. His master, as everybody knows, has treated him most shamefully."

"The horse shall have justice!" agreed the other judges.

By then, a crowd of men and women and children had gathered in the marketplace and stood wondering at the horse. They were full of tales of how they had seen him wandering on the hills, unfed, uncared for, while his master sat at home counting his bags of gold.

"Go bring the miser before us," said the judges.

And when he came, they bade him stand and hear their judgement.

"This horse has served you well for many a year," they said. "He has saved you from many a peril. He has helped you gain your wealth. Therefore we order that one half of all your gold shall be set aside to buy him shelter and food, a green pasture in which he may graze, and a warm stall to comfort him in his old age."

The miser hung his head and grieved to lose his gold, but the people shouted with joy. The horse was led away to his new stall and a dinner such as he had not had in many a day.

About the Artists

Simon Mendez

Simon lives and works in Yorkshire, England, and has always loved to draw. His father, an illustrator and designer, has been an inspiration to him. Simon concentrates mostly on portraits and animal subjects. In his spare time he reads biographies, watches movies and enjoys walks in the countryside.

Cover illustration

Iole Rosa

Iole has loved drawing nature, especially animals, since she was a small child. At college she specialized in illustration, but her career began as a graphic designer. In 2002 she moved into the world of children's books and began illustrating full time. Iole lives in Formello, Rome, with her six cats.

Into the Saddle

Mélanie Florian

French illustrator Mélanie has always had a passion for drawing and telling stories. Her favourite medium is watercolour, for the freshness, lightness and freedom it offers. Her work has been published worldwide, and she has also written and illustrated two books that have been published in several countries.

Noble Steeds

Gail Yerrill

Gail has been illustrating stories from an early age. She loves to create characters and worlds where marvellous things happen. She is known for her soft, cute style and fresh watercolours, and she loves to experiment with new techniques, colours and texture. Her work has been published all over the world.

Ride like the Wind

Kirsteen Harris-Jones

After leaving college, Kirsteen worked as a graphic designer at various design studios. She then went freelance, and after having two children, went back to Glyndwr University to study illustration for publishing. After having her third child she joined The Bright Agency, and is now constantly busy.

Adventures on Horseback

Frank Endersby

Frank's earliest memory is sitting in his high chair as a child, drawing a train. This love for illustration led to a career in art and design, and Frank has produced greeting cards, picture prints and even toys. His work has been been published across the globe, and has won awards in both the USA and Israel.

Home Free